CHILDRENS
RESERVE
COLLECTION

MANY LIBRARIES IN ESSEX HAVE
FACILITIES FOR EXHIBITIONS AND
MEETINGS — ENQUIRE AT YOUR
LOCAL LIBRARY FOR DETAILS

D1491773

SERRAILLIER, IAN
THE IVORY HORN. RETOLD FROM
THE SONG OF ROLAND.
JF

30130 128493094

THE IVORY HORN

The Song of Roland

THE IVORY HORN

RETOLD FROM

The Song of Roland

IAN SERRAILLIER

ILLUSTRATED BY WILLIAM STOBBS

LONDON
OXFORD UNIVERSITY PRESS

JF

BJ 93712

© IAN SERRAILLIER 1960

FIRST PUBLISHED
1960
Reprinted 1967

Oxford University Press, Ely House, London W. 1
GLASGOW NEW YORK TORONTO MELBOURNE WELLINGTON
CAPE TOWN SALISBURY IBADAN NAIROBI LUSAKA ADDIS ABABA
BOMBAY CALCUTTA MADRAS KARACHI LAHORE DACCA
KUALA LUMPUR HONG KONG TOKYO

PRINTED IN GREAT BRITAIN BY
WESTERN PRINTING SERVICES LTD BRISTOL

To Jane

Contents

Introduction

ON 15TH AUGUST, 778, the Emperor Charlemagne and his army were crossing the
Pyrenees on their way back to France. They
had been fighting the Saracens in Spain. As the
rearguard was passing through the narrow valley of
Roncesvalles, from the wooded slopes of the mountains a treacherous party of Basques swept down
upon them, looted their baggage and slaughtered
every man. Writing some fifty years later, a chroni-
cler reports that Roland, Duke of the Marches of
Brittany, was one of the many slain.

Such is the historical basis for the epic poem *The
Song of Roland*, which was not written till some two
centuries later. By this time legend and the imagination of a poet have transformed a comparatively
unimportant episode into a major drama. In 778
Charlemagne was only thirty-eight. But the poet

makes him a majestic figure of great age, more than two hundred years old. Instead of the Basques we have the infidel Saracens, and Charlemagne is the champion of Christendom against them. He is a mighty warrior whose conquests extend throughout Europe, from Lombardy to Scotland, from Bavaria to Spain. Nevertheless it is not he but his nephew Roland who is the hero of the story. Legend gives Roland the command of the rearguard. Oliver, his companion in arms, Archbishop Turpin of Rheims, and the other nine Peers of France go with him and share his exploits. To avoid any stain on French honour, there must be a scapegoat for the disaster of Roncesvalles. This is the rôle of Ganelon, Roland's stepfather, who is in league with the Saracen King, Marsila. Ganelon is a purely fictitious figure, but without him the story would lose its drama and excitement and much of its poignancy.

Most people are familiar with the story of Roncesvalles and of the sounding of the horn, but the epic does not—as some modern versions might suggest—end here. The events that follow it—Charlemagne's revenge on the Saracens, and the trial and downfall of Ganelon—are needed to complete the plot and are no less interesting and exciting. The feudal audience for whom the poem was originally composed would have been left puzzled and unsatisfied by any story which stopped short at Roland's death and did not include the revenge. It helps our own enjoyment of it to realize what sort of people they were and to know something about the times they lived in, for it is the spirit of the eleventh and not the eighth century that the poem reflects.

The social structure was based on vassalage. In return for service and devotion, the vassal could count on his lord's protection. As Dorothy Sayers writes in the introduction to her translation of the poem, 'it was the duty of every great lord to serve the King in battle, bringing with him so many armed vassals, each of whom brought so many lesser vassals of his own, and so on down the whole scale of hierarchy'. Each vassal owed allegiance to his lord until death. At a time when most people were illiterate, tokens like gloves and staffs were more common than written agreements and messages. Thus, when Ganelon takes Charlemagne's message to Marsila, he carries the Emperor's glove and staff as a symbol of his authority. The glove is also used for two other purposes: as a challenge to combat and to mark a gift of land or even a kingdom. At the trial of Ganelon, Pinabel and Thierry each hand a glove to the Emperor, pledging themselves to fight each other. When the dying Marsila surrenders his glove to his overlord the Emir Baligant, he is returning the lands and kingdoms given to him before.

As Dorothy Sayers writes, it was an 'unsophisticated period, when the extreme insecurity of life made martial prowess the most necessary of manly virtues, and it was every baron's business to be a tower of strength to the dwellers on his own land'. The noblest qualities were courage, loyalty and self-sacrifice; the unforgivable crime, treachery. In times of rejoicing or in the face of death and disaster it was considered quite natural to give full expression to one's feelings. Thus, when Charlemagne finds Roland's body on the battlefield, he does not attempt to master his emotions. 'With a cry he leapt down from his horse and took Roland's head between his hands. Dazed with grief, he swooned away.' And his army swooned in sympathy with his distress! There was nothing incongruous or unmanly in weeping openly, and valiant soldiers would shed tears without shame.

In such a world Roland himself, proud, courageous and rash, seeing all issues in the simplest terms of black and white, is the ideal hero. When he lay dying, after a life wholly dedicated to glory and to battle, he thought for a while of his many victories, of his country and his kinsmen, and 'above all of Charlemagne his lord and Emperor who had brought him up from childhood in his own household'. His last act was to turn towards Spain, so that Charlemagne should see that he had died with his face to the foe, his last words to ask God to forgive his sins and receive his soul. For these proud soldiers there was nothing inconsistent in the mingling of Christianity and warfare. Archbishop Turpin of Rheims, the brave, sensible and unselfish warrior-priest, blesses his troops before battle and assures them that if they are slain they will go straight to Paradise and dwell with the Innocents for ever. Not only does he fight himself, but he is given the signal honour of opening the battle. He seems to regard the life of the cloister as far inferior to that of combat, and one can almost hear his axiom that the best Christian is the one who kills the most pagans. In the different world of today such a conception of Christianity would seem to us naïve and misguided, but in the century of the First Crusade, when

Christendom saw itself threatened by the Moslem world, such an attitude was understandable and perhaps inevitable.

War is the background of the whole story. In the eleventh century it seems to have been a more chivalrous business than modern warfare, with a code of conduct that was strictly observed. The poet of *The Song of Roland* depicts it as a series of individual combats, and the pattern on which they are based is quite clear. They were fought on horseback, and if you wanted to avoid being trampled to death in the press of battle you had to stay mounted. The saddle, as we can see from the Bayeux tapestry, was designed to keep you firmly in position. It had long stirrups—when Roland faints, they prevent him from falling—and a padded seat with high bows in front and behind. If the saddle-girth broke, you fell to the ground. The fight began with a threat or insult from the challenger, as when Adelroth, Marsila's nephew, threatens Roland at the beginning of the Battle of Roncesvalles. The combatants then charged, holding their spears, which often carried pennons below the point, firmly under their arms. The object was to pierce through an opponent's breast or unsaddle him by sheer weight and speed. If both spears were shattered, they drew their swords and, using the edge and not the point, hacked away at each other's heads. For a really heavy blow they grasped the hilt with both hands. If the combatants were unhorsed, the fight continued on foot in the same way. In a long fight they would pause for breath and summon each other to repent and surrender. This happens when Charlemagne and Baligant meet. If both refused, they fought on till one of them was killed. In *The Song of Roland* no prisoners were taken. When your enemy was safely dead, you called him a rude name and hurled his body contemptuously aside. Such, then, was the pattern, and the poet sees that its form is carefully observed. His audience would have been as shocked by the foul blow that kills Oliver as we should be today if, during a boxing championship, we saw one of the boxers suddenly kick his opponent in the face.

Lastly, a word about my retelling. I intended originally to attempt it in verse, but I found this too restricting. Even in prose it has not been an easy task. The larger canvas made it possible to keep more of the story, and, considered purely as a tale of heroic adventure, the plot could hardly be bettered. But mere story-telling, however brisk or accurate, is not enough—there is more than this to *The Song of Roland*. It is an epic poem intended, like *Beowulf*, to be spoken aloud. According to tradition, the minstrel Taillefer in William the Conqueror's army sang part of it at the Battle of Hastings. I have tried therefore to use language which can, especially in the dialogue, be comfortably spoken aloud without sounding too stilted. The original poem is deeply moving; it has passion and pathos, gentleness and horror, and above all a rich humanity. My version cannot hope to be more than a faint echo, but if there is a spark or two left from which the imagination can take fire I shall be satisfied.

I

King Marsila's Council

FOR SEVEN LONG years the mighty Charlemagne, Emperor of France and champion of Christendom, had been fighting the Moslems in Spain. He had gathered his army from all over the Empire—from Lombardy in the south to Denmark in the north, from Brittany to the Baltic. There were men from the valleys of the Moselle and the Rhine and from the forests of Bavaria, Flemings from the Lowlands, and from the provinces of France the bravest battalions of all, the very flower of knighthood. In seven years he had taken all the highlands as far as the sea, captured every castle, breached every wall and broken the cities—all save one, Saragossa, safe on its crown of rock. Marsila, King of Spain, still clung to it—Marsila, Christ's enemy, sworn servant of Mohammed; God strike him down!

One day King Marsila was reclining in his orchard on a bench of blue marble with twenty thousand pagans at his feet. Vexed in spirit, brooding on his cares, he summoned his barons before him.

'My noble lords,' he said, 'I need not tell you what trouble we are in. Since Charlemagne, Emperor of France, bore down on our country, we have been thrown to the wild waters, plunged in misery after misery. What are we to do? I have no army to match his. Must we be swept away to death and disgrace?'

The pagans were silent, pondering his words.

Then, in the quiet and the stillness a voice rang out. It was Blancandrin, a brave knight and the wiliest counsellor among them.

'Sir, do not distress yourself,' he said. 'There is no need to be afraid. You must make a treaty with Charlemagne, a treaty of false friendship. Promise to load him with gifts—lions, prancing bears, greyhounds swift as arrows, a train of camels seven hundred strong, a thousand hawks with trim and glittering feathers, twice two hundred pack-mules, their panniers bursting with silver and gold—yes, send him all these, if he will return to France. With so much treasure he can pay his soldiers proudly— they must be sick of fighting and eager to return home. Further, you must promise to go to France yourself at Michaelmas to be baptized a Christian and swear yourself his liegeman. Should he ask for hostages, then send him our own sons. Some ten or twenty will do, and I'll willingly send mine. Better to risk their necks than our honour. It's a good bait —he is sure to take it. Sir, these Frenchmen will return to their land at once—by my right hand I swear it, by the beard that blows on my chest!— and Michaelmas will pass and you will still be in Spain. But we must be ready to lose our sons, for Charlemagne has a cruel and stubborn heart and is sure to have their heads. Even that would be better than to lose Spain.'

'Well spoken,' said the pagans.

When the council was over, King Marsila sought out his ten most rascally knights and called them to him. They were steeped in villainy and the black ways of wickedness—and Blancandrin was one of them.

'My lords,' said the King, 'go now to Cordova— Charlemagne is besieging it with his engines of war. Carry olive branches in your hands as tokens of peace. If you fix this treaty, I will reward you well, be sure of that.'

He sent for ten white mules, dazzling creatures, their saddles set in silver, their bridles of gleaming gold. And the knights mounted and rode away to do his bidding.

II

Charlemagne's Council

CHARLEMAGNE HAD CAPTURED Cordova, and
his heart was happy as a mountain river
laughing and leaping in the sun. He had
breached the walls, tumbled the towers with his
engines of war, and won vast plunder of silver and
gold. He had baptized all the pagans or struck them
dead with the sword.

When Marsila's messengers arrived, the Emperor
was in his orchard, sheltering from the fierce heat

of the sun. Roland and Oliver were with him; so were Duke Samson, Geoffrey of Anjou, his standard-bearer, and fifteen thousand soldiers. The knights were dallying on carpets of white silk, the old at chess, the young at sword-play. In the shade of a pine tree, near a bush of wild roses whose fragrance filled the air, there was a golden throne. And here the Emperor was sitting, a magnificent figure with his proud face and upright bearing, his lion's mane of waving hair, and his beard as white as the may-blossom.

The ten messengers dismounted and stood before him, the olive branches in their hands, and on their lips greetings of love and goodwill.

With many a flowered phrase and honeyed promise, Blancandrin delivered King Marsila's message.

Charlemagne listened with bowed head, probing in the pool of words for hidden treacheries. He was never hasty, but calm and deliberate in speech and counsel.

'Marsila is my enemy,' he said. 'How do I know I can trust him?'

'We are willing to send you hostages,' said Blancandrin, 'ten, fifteen or twenty. My own son will be one of them, though I risk sending him to his death, and others of even nobler birth. At Michaelmas you will be back in your palace at Aix, and my King will follow you there to be baptized.'

'He may still save his soul,' said Charlemagne.

The evening was cloudless and the sun shining in all his glory. The Emperor had the mules stabled.

He provided the messengers with a tent in the orchard and twelve servants to wait on them. And they slept there all night.

In the first light of morning he rose and, after hearing Mass and Matins, went to his throne under the pine tree. Then he summoned his barons to finish his council, for he always listened to their advice. Duke Oger of Denmark came, and Turpin, Archbishop of Rheims; Richard the Old and his nephew Henry, and the rest of the Twelve Peers of France. Roland was there and gentle, courteous Oliver. Roland was the Emperor's nephew, brought up in the royal household and loved like a son. According to the custom of the day, Roland and Oliver had been companions since childhood, trained together in arms and horsemanship, in learning and good manners, sharing all things together. And the ties that bound them to each other and to Charlemagne their overlord were as strong as those of blood or marriage.

At once the Emperor began his council. It was to bring them grief and disaster, for among the thousand Frenchmen present was the traitor Ganelon.

'My lord barons,' said the Emperor, 'I need your advice. King Marsila has promised me fine gifts—lions, prancing bears, greyhounds swift as arrows, a train of camels seven hundred strong, a thousand hawks with trim and glittering plumage, twice two hundred pack-mules, their panniers bursting with silver and gold—if only we return to France. He swears to come himself and be baptized. Tell me, is his heart in this?'

'Take care!' cried the French. And their voice was like the shudder of ten thousand starlings rising in terror from the fields, darkening the air.

Roland sprang to his feet.

'He means treachery,' he said. 'You can never trust him. Remember, once before he sued for peace and sent fifteen pagans with olive branches and the same cringing words. You fell into the trap and sent two envoys to arrange a truce, Basile and Basan, both of them nobles. How did Marsila show good faith? By lopping off their heads. You cannot end the war till you've avenged their deaths. March on Saragossa, lay siege to it with all your heart and strength.'

The Emperor bowed his head. He plucked his beard wildly, but answered not a word.

Then Ganelon leapt up and stood in front of him.

'There is no sense in what Roland says—don't listen to him,' he cried. 'Marsila is willing to make peace and to hold Spain as your liegeman. The offer is sincere, you stand to gain by it. Only a reckless fool and a gambler would throw it back at him.'

Duke Naimon, the wisest of the Emperor's counsellors, spoke next.

'You have thrashed Marsila in battle,' he said, 'breached his walls, tumbled his towers with your engines of war, burnt his cities, beaten his men— what more do you want? He asks for mercy. Send one of your barons to test his good faith. If he is truly sincere, then this terrible war can be ended.'

'Wisely spoken,' said the French.

'My lord barons,' said the Emperor, 'whom shall we send to Saragossa to King Marsila?'

'I beg you to send me,' said Duke Naimon. 'Give me the glove and the staff.'

'I need your counsel here,' said the Emperor. 'By my beard, you shall not go so far away.'

'Let me go,' said Roland.

'That would never do,' said Oliver. 'You're too headstrong and quarrelsome. It would be safer for the Emperor to send me.'

'Silence, both of you!' said Charlemagne. 'Neither of you shall go. By my white beard, anyone who dares to name one of my Twelve Peers shall pay for it.'

The French said nothing. The Emperor's words had shamed them into silence.

Then Turpin, Archbishop of Rheims, got up.

'Sir, you have been in this country seven years,' he said. 'Your armies have endured continuous hardship and terror—they need a rest. Give me the glove and the staff. Let me go.'

The Emperor answered him angrily, 'Silence, Turpin! Go back to your silk carpet till I call on you to speak.' He looked round on his nobles. 'Knights of France,' he commanded, 'choose me a baron to carry my message to King Marsila.'

'Ganelon, my stepfather,' said Roland. 'Let him take it.'

'Ganelon! Ganelon!' echoed the French. 'He's the man for us.'

But Ganelon was furious. He threw off his cloak of marten fur and bared his silken shirt. His face was defiant, his eyes bright with fire; his shoulders, broad and magnificent, made pygmies of them all.

'Madman and idiot!' he cried. 'You are sending me to my death. If ever I come back alive, I shall hound you with hatred to the grave.'

'Braggart, I'm not afraid of your threats,' said Roland. 'This is no light errand, it calls for some skill. If the Emperor agrees, I'm quite ready to do it for you.'

'Never,' cried Ganelon. 'You are not my liege-man nor I your lord. The Emperor has chosen me and I shall go to Saragossa. But I despise and detest you for what you have done. And I warn you, this is not the last you'll hear of it.'

But Roland only laughed in his face—laughed with such open mockery that Ganelon exploded with rage.

'By Heaven you shall pay for this, Roland,' he said. 'You picked me out of spite.' He turned to Charlemagne. 'Royal Emperor, I'm ready to obey your command. I shall go to Saragossa. I know that whoever goes there has no hope of return. First, I would like to ask a favour of you. My wife— your sister, sir—bore me a son. His name is Baldwin and he is the finest son that a father could wish for. I leave him my lands and my living. Look after him, for he is your kinsman and I shall never see him again.'

'You are too anxious,' said Charlemagne. 'But you have heard my orders and you must go. Take the glove and the staff, for the French have chosen—'

'Sir, it was Roland who chose me, not the French,'

said Ganelon. 'I shall hate him for the rest of my life, and Oliver his companion, and the other Peers who dote on him so. I defy the whole pack of them.'

'You are too passionate,' said Charlemagne. 'But you have heard my orders and you must go.'

'I go alone,' said Ganelon bitterly, 'alone, with no one to protect me—like Basan and Basile before me. And we know what happened to them.'

The Emperor handed him his glove. As Ganelon reached forward to grasp it, it fell to the ground.

The traitor smarted with shame.

The French shouted, 'God, what trick of fate is this, what grim foreboding of disaster?' And their voice was like the rumble of thunder in the mountains.

'You shall learn soon enough,' said Ganelon, stooping to pick up the glove. Then he turned to the Emperor. 'Have I your leave to go now? There's nothing to keep me here.'

'Go, in Christ's Name,' said Charlemagne. He gave him the staff and the letter.

And away went Ganelon, with the glove and the staff and the letter and the Emperor's blessing.

III

Ganelon's Treachery

GANELON HURRIED TO his lodging and ar-
rayed himself in great splendour for his
journey. He fastened spurs of gold to his feet
and clapped his sword Killbane to his side. Then he
mounted his horse Firebrand, while his uncle held
the stirrup. There was a great hustling of knights
round him.

'This is a poor reward for your courage,' they
said. 'You are a splendid soldier, of noble family;

you have served in the King's court for many years.
Roland had no right to treat you so harshly.' And
they begged him with tears to take them with him.

But Ganelon refused. 'I would rather die alone
than drag you down with me. You shall live and
return home to France. Send greetings to my wife,
to my friend Pinabel and Baldwin my son. I leave
him in your hands. I know you will look after
him.'

He took the road through the wood of olive trees
and soon caught up with the pagan envoys. Blancandrin dropped behind to keep him company, and
they talked to each other with infinite cunning.

'Your Emperor is a man of miracles,' said Blancandrin. 'His conquests reach as far as England.
What does he want here with us?'

'It is his will and pleasure,' said Ganelon. 'There
is no king in the world to match him.'

'The French are brave men,' said Blancandrin,
'but the advice that their barons offer Charlemagne is mere mischief.'

'Which barons do you mean?' asked Ganelon.
'I can think of none to condemn—unless you mean
Roland, and he is doomed. A few mornings ago,
when the Emperor was sitting in his orchard, along
came his nephew still wearing his coat of mail—
he was just back from some raid or other. He had
a golden apple in his hand and showed it to the
Emperor. "Take it, sir," he said with a flourish,
"my gift to you, the crown of all kings."' Ganelon shuddered. 'Roland's arrogance will destroy
him. There can be no peace while he lives.'

'He is a hard man,' said Blancandrin. 'He wants to trample every nation under his heel—but where will he find enough support?'

'The French will not fail him—they love him too well, for he makes them presents of silver and gold, mules, war horses, and clothes of fine silk. He will conquer every country in the world.'

Scheming and gossiping, by lane and track and leafy wood they rode together. And they swore eternal loyalty to each other—and death to Roland.

At last they came to Saragossa and dismounted. The sun was like a furnace, and they were scorched and weary after the long journey.

In the shade of a pine tree they saw a throne draped and canopied with silk of Alexandria. Marsila, King of Spain, was sitting on it. He had a gold-feathered dart in his hand and twenty thousand Saracens at his feet, silent in the stillness, thirsty for news.

Blancandrin took Ganelon by the hand and led him to the King.

'Greeting, sir, in the name of Mohammed whose faith we hold!' said Blancandrin. 'I have delivered your message to Charlemagne.'

'How did he receive it?' asked the King, and he leaned forward eagerly.

'He lifted both hands to Heaven and praised his God,' said Blancandrin. 'That was all the answer he gave me. But he has sent you here a noble lord, Count Ganelon of France, who shall tell you whether you will have peace or not.'

'Let him speak,' said King Marsila.

Then Ganelon, choosing words that had lain long simmering in his mind, with careful cunning addressed the pagan King:

'Greeting, sir, in the Name of God Almighty, whom all the world should worship! This is the message great Charlemagne sends you: if you are baptized a Christian, he will give you half Spain. Refuse him, and he shall bind you in chains. The ugliest pack-mule will cart you off to Aix, and you shall die there in squalor and disgrace.'

The colour fled from King Marsila's cheeks, the gold-feathered dart trembled in his hand. He would have hurled it at Ganelon, but the pagans held him back and pressed him to his throne.

Then the Caliph, the King's uncle, cried out, 'You put us in the wrong if you strike the man. You should be patient and listen.'

'I am not afraid,' said Ganelon, who had plucked his sword two fingers' length from the scabbard. 'For all God's gold, for all the teeming wealth of your land, I will not withhold one word of my Emperor's message. He is your enemy until death.'

Tearing off his silk scarf and his cloak of marten's fur, he flung them to the ground. Blancandrin picked them up. But Ganelon would not let go of his sword. He clutched the golden hilt tight in his fist, while the pagans marvelled at his spirit. Then he went up to the King and scornfully handed him the Emperor's message.

Marsila broke the seal and threw away the wax. As he read the letter, his eyes blazed with anger.

'The killing of Basan and Basile—he dares throw

that in my teeth!' he cried. 'He tells me to send him my uncle the Caliph as recompense!'

'What insolence!' said Jurfaret, the King's son. 'Ganelon has gone too far and must die for this.' His right hand ran to his sword hilt.

But Ganelon was too quick for him. He drew his steel and brandished it above his head. With his eyes flashing fire, he stood back against a pine tree, ready to strike at Jurfaret if he stirred an inch. The pagans sprang upon both and held them back. In a fury of rage Marsila stamped off to his orchard, quickly followed by his uncle, his son and Blancandrin.

Out of the bright sunshine in the cool of the trees, Blancandrin did his best to calm him. 'Send for the Frenchman,' he urged. 'He has sworn to be loyal to me and support our cause.'

By the time Ganelon was brought, the King had regained his calm.

'Ganelon, I was wrong to raise my hand against you,' he said. 'I spoke too hastily. To make amends, I'll give you these skins of marten fur tomorrow. They're worth five hundred pounds.'

'I never refuse a gift like that,' said Ganelon, smiling his thanks.

'I begin to like you,' said the King. 'Come and sit beside me and tell me of Charlemagne.'

'His deeds of glory are brighter than the sun,' said Ganelon. 'He would rather die than fail his country.'

'But he is weary and old now—more than two hundred years old,' said King Marsila. 'He has fought in many lands and made beggars of rich kings. His shield has been battered with a thousand blows. Will he never be tired of fighting?'

'Not while Roland is alive. There are no greater soldiers under Heaven than he and Oliver. He dotes on them and on the other Peers of France. And his vanguard is twenty thousand strong.'

'I can put ten—twenty times that number in the field——'

'And lose the lot if you leave Roland alive,' said Ganelon. 'Now, listen. I can tell you how to bring Charlemagne to his knees. Send him the treasure you promised him and the twenty hostages. He will return to France and leave his rearguard behind in the Pass of Roncesvalles at the very gates of Spain. I'll see that Roland stays behind with the rearguard, and Oliver as well. You can trap them in the Pass and kill both of them.'

'That's easily said, but I may miss them—they may escape my clutches,' said Marsila.

But Ganelon had his plan ready. With no hint of hesitation he answered, 'Divide your army into two. Send the first hundred thousand to cut down as many of the French as they can, then send a second army to finish off the rest. Believe me, Roland cannot escape both. Roland is the Emperor's right arm, and Spain will not be at peace till he is dead.'

Ganelon's plan pleased Marsila. The King embraced him and said, 'We need waste no more words. Give me your oath now, swear to betray Roland.'

So Ganelon, grasping the jewelled hilt of Killbane

as it gleamed and sparkled in the sunshine, swore his shameless treason. Then Marsila had the holy book of Mohammed brought to him. He placed his hand on it and swore that when he found Roland he would do his best to kill him.

Several knights brought presents to Ganelon. Valdebron came first.

'Take my sword,' he said. 'A thousand gold sovereigns lie bedded in the hilt. Is it heavy enough for Roland's head?'

Laughing they kissed on chin and cheek.

Climorin gave his helmet, the toughest one in the world.

'Take it, wear it,' he said, 'for Roland may get his blow in first.'

Laughing they kissed on chin and cheek.

Bramimunde, Queen of Spain, came next.

'My heart goes out to you,' she said, 'because my lord and all his host esteem you so highly. Here are two gold necklaces for your wife. They are set with rubies and amethysts and are worth more than all the wealth of Rome. Your Emperor has nothing as fine as these.'

Ganelon put them in his pocket.

Then the King called Malduit, his treasurer.

'Are the gifts for Charlemagne ready?' he asked.

'Yes, sir. Seven hundred camels laden with silver and gold.'

'And the hostages?'

'They are waiting—twenty of them, picked from the noblest families.'

Marsila laid his hand on Ganelon's shoulder.

'You have acted very wisely,' he said. 'By the faith you Christians hold dear, see that you keep your promises. You deserve a rich reward. I'll send you ten treasure-mules laden with Arabian gold, and every year ten more like them. Meanwhile, take the keys of our city with you and open its gates to Charlemagne. And do not fail to see that Roland is in the rearguard at Roncesvalles. You can leave the rest to me.'

Ganelon mounted his horse. With triumph ringing in his heart, he galloped back to the French.

IV

Charlemagne returns to France

CHARLEMAGNE WAS ON his way back to France when, one morning in the waking light, Ganelon rode into his camp. The Emperor was standing on the grass in front of his tent with Roland, Oliver and Duke Naimon.

'Greeting to you, sir, in God's Name,' said Ganelon. 'I bring you the keys of Saragossa and all the treasure that your heart could wish.'

'Where are the twenty hostages?' said Charlemagne.

'You have nothing to fear. They are on the road.'

'Is the Caliph among them?' asked the Emperor.

'The Caliph is dead,' said Ganelon. And from the bottomless pit of his cunning he drew this story: 'When the pagan King promised to become a Christian, the Caliph was furious and fled to the coast. He put out to sea with an army four hundred thousand strong, armed with shield and helmet and coat of mail, their jewel-hilted swords buckled to their sides—with my own eyes I saw them go. They were barely four leagues out when the sky grew dark and the wind blew loud and the storm-wave swallowed them. He will never trouble you again—and neither will King Marsila. Before a month is past he will follow you to France and become a Christian; he will be your liegeman and hold from you the kingdom of Spain.'

'God bless you for this,' said Charlemagne. 'You have done bravely, Ganelon, and I shall reward you well.' The cares faded from his face, and he smiled. Then in a ringing voice he cried, 'Sound all the trumpets! Load the beasts of burden, break camp—for the war is ended!'

And they took the road that wound through the great valleys to France.

Sitting proudly in his saddle, Charlemagne re-called his many triumphs—the castles he had captured, the walls he had breached, the great cities he had broken—and his heart bounded like a mountain river laughing and leaping in the sun.

Meanwhile King Marsila had been preparing for war. From the farthest borders of his kingdom he had summoned his barons, the sons of his earls, his

counts and viscounts—the flower of all Spain—and in three days had gathered together an army of four hundred thousand. They beat the drums in Saragossa, they set an image of Mohammed on the topmost tower of the city and lifted their eyes in prayer to him. Then they mounted their horses and were soon on the march through the mountains. They were armed with shield and helmet and coat of mail, their jewel-hilted swords buckled to their sides, the pennons on their lances streaming in the wind. And towards nightfall they camped on a wooded hill-top and lay down to wait for the dawn.

But Charlemagne knew nothing of this.

The sun sank down and darkness covered the hills. In the cool and the stillness of the night the Emperor lay sleeping, dreaming that he was at the great Pass of Sizer with his spear of ashwood in his hand. Suddenly Ganelon snatched it from his fist so fiercely that it snapped and the splinters shivered to the stars. . . . But Charlemagne slept on without waking.

His sleep was troubled with another dream. He was in his chapel at Aix when a bear bit his arm and a leopard sprang upon him and would have savaged him had not a greyhound leapt from the shadows to fight them back. Long and furiously they tussled, but there was no telling which would win. . . .

Charlemagne slept on without waking—till dawn, till the first light roused him and the warmth of day crept back into the hills. But the gloom of his dream remained with him. Anxious to dispel it, he mounted his horse and rode proudly through his ranks. And soon, in the presence of their might, his fears melted as dew-mist in the morning sun.

'Sound the trumpets!' he commanded.

And all the trumpets sounded, echoing from peak to peak.

When the last echo had died away he halted. Gazing far out over the hills, he cried, 'Lord barons, we are near the Gates of Spain, at the Pass of Roncesvalles whose narrow windings will lead us home to France. We must leave a rearguard behind to cover our going. Choose me a leader to command it.'

Before anyone could answer, Ganelon spoke out: 'Roland my stepson. I choose him for his valour.'

'Madman, you choose him out of spite!' cried Charlemagne, and his eyes were angry as the raging sea.

Roland did not flinch from the challenge. 'Sir, my stepfather does me a great honour,' he said. 'Every steed and saddle-beast, every palfrey and pack-horse that is lost will be paid for in blood. I shall not disgrace you.'

'True,' said Ganelon quickly. 'That is no idle boast.'

But Roland rounded upon his stepfather. 'Son of a slut!' he shouted. 'When the Emperor gives me his bow, do you expect me to drop it as you dropped his glove?' He turned to Charlemagne. 'Sir, give me the bow you are holding. I shall not let it fall.'

The Emperor drew back; he dared not look him in the face. In torment of spirit he plucked his beard, and the tears burst from his eyes.

Then Duke Naimon, the wisest of his counsellors, gave his advice.

'Sir, you see how angry Roland is. But he has been clearly chosen and there can be no turning back.' And with gentle firmness he added, 'You must forget your fears and give him the bow.'

The Emperor raised his head and, leaning forward, gave Roland the bow.

'He must have all the support he needs,' said the Duke.

'Roland, you shall have half my army,' said the Emperor.

'That is more than I need,' said Roland. 'Twenty thousand Frenchmen are enough. Keep the rest to see you safely through the Gates of Spain, and so long as I live you need fear no enemy.' He called Oliver to him and the Peers of France.

'I will go with him too,' said Archbishop Turpin. 'And I,' said Count Walter. 'I am Roland's man.' Between them they picked their twenty thousand.

'Count Walter,' said Roland when all was ready, 'take a thousand of my best men and hold the gorges and the heights on our flank.'

They were chosen, and he watched them climb by a steep track that zig-zagged up the mountain-side. Soon they were on the ridge-top, tiny specks against the sky.

Then Charlemagne embraced his nephew. He clung to his neck and wept bitterly as he bade him farewell. As he rode to the head of his army he did not glance back. Defiant and resolute, he set his face towards Roncesvalles and France.

Slowly the shadows of the great Pass lengthened, devouring the afternoon sunlight, devouring the last of that huge army. The sun still lingered on the heights, firing the hills and the tree-tops with golden light. But the valley where Roland stood, gazing sadly into the mouth of the Pass, was full of shadows and a chill wind was blowing.

High are the hills, deep and dark are the valleys, grim are the rocks and the narrow passes full of fear. As the French rode through the Pass of Roncesvalles, their spirits sank—they could not endure the desolation of the place. Every rider spurred on his horse, every driver cracked his whip. On groaning axle, on hoof and hurrying wheel they sped fast and ever faster, louder and louder. Fifteen leagues away you could hear the thunder of their passing. When at last they drew near to the Great Land of France,

in sight of Gascony, the pace slackened. And their
spirits rose—like a flock of birds from a field, rushing
the heights of the boundless sky. They thought of
homes and wives and lovers, and the tears sprang
to their eyes. But none was more moved than

Charlemagne, who had left his nephew Roland at the Gates of Spain. And he covered his head with a cloak to hide his tears.

'Sir, why are you so distressed?' said Duke Naimon as he rode beside him, and he searched his master's troubled face.

'Must you ask?' said Charlemagne, and his voice was choked with sorrow. 'It is because Ganelon is going to break our great nation. Last night as I lay sleeping, I dreamed that he snatched my spear of ashwood from my hand so fiercely that it snapped and the splinters shivered to the stars. It was he that chose Roland for the rearguard, and I have left him in a strange land. God, if I lose him, who in the wide world can take his place?'

A hundred thousand French hearts trembled in grief and fear for Roland.

In all that vast company one man alone was happy—the traitor Ganelon. He was thinking of the treasure Marsila had given him—silver and gold, silk coats and crimson carpets, mules, horses, lions, camels by the hundred. And his rascal heart rejoiced.

V

The Saracens prepare for Battle

WITH THE DAWN Marsila's army was soon
pressing on through the long valleys—four
hundred thousand men marching, marching.

In the afternoon one of their scouts, who had
ranged far ahead of the rest, galloped down from a
hill-top and reported to the King.

'The French are in the next valley. I have seen
their pennons flying—purple, emerald and flaming

gold. The rearguard of the Twelve Peers is ready for battle.'

'So Roland's hour is near,' said the King.

'Let me be the first to strike him,' said his nephew Adelroth, drawing rein in front of him. 'Kill Roland, and from the headlands of the south to the northern Gates, Spain will be clear of the invader. Sir, grant me that honour.'

'I grant it willingly. You were always first in the field,' said the King, and he gave him his glove.

His nephew waved it above his head. 'A princely gift! An honour beyond all honours!' he cried. 'But I cannot take on the Twelve Peers of France single-handed. I need twelve barons to match them—who are they to be?'

The King's brother Fulsaron was the first to come forward, and others followed quickly: Corsalis King of Barbary, a fearless warrior steeped in villainy and the black ways of wickedness; the Prince of Brigant, who could run faster than a horse; Margaris of Seville, so gallant and handsome that all the ladies of Spain sighed for his kisses; Chernible, who came from a land of devils that grew no living thing, where there was neither sun nor rain nor dew and every stone was black. His hair hung down to the ground and he was so tough that he could carry four laden mules on his back. These and six others stepped forward, each more cruel-hearted than the last.

And they vowed to kill Roland.

'We shall plunge our swords into him,' said Fulsaron.

'And stain them red with his blood,' said Corsalis.

'The Emperor loves him with all his heart,' said the Prince of Brigant. 'He is too old to bear this loss—he will carry his grief to the grave.'

'Too old? He staggers under his years like a top-heavy pack-mule,' scoffed Margaris.

'A mule with a beard as white as the may-blossom,' said Chernible. 'We shall trample it in the dirt.'

The Saracens laced up their helmets and armed themselves with shields and triple thickness of mail. Their swords were of true Vienna steel, their lances tipped with pennons, white and blue and scarlet-red. Stepping from their mules, they mounted their war horses and, with their armour ablaze like a forest fire, rode in close company under the shining sun. And a thousand trumpets rang their happiness to high Heaven.

Far away in the Pass of Roncesvalles the French heard the sound.

'Listen! The pagans are coming,' said Oliver. 'We shall fight them after all.'

'God grant we may,' said Roland, and his soul was deeply stirred. 'We must stand here for our Emperor. Our cause is just. It is right that a man should suffer for his lord. He should endure winter snow and the scorch of summer and wear himself to the bone in his service. The pagans are wrong, we Christians are right, and I shall set an example all France will be proud of.'

Then Oliver climbed to the top of a high mountain and, looking down far into the kingdom of Spain, saw the pagan army marching. The sun was shining on their jewelled helmets, their shields and coats of mail, their spears and their streaming pennons, and they were numberless as the waves of the sea. In great dismay he ran down from the mountain and told the French what he had seen.

'I could not count their divisions,' he said. 'No one ever saw such an army—a hundred thousand soldiers at least. What a battle it will be! Stand fast and may God be your strength and shield!'

'And may He hate all cowards!' cried the French. 'We shall not fail you.'

'A word with you, Roland,' said Oliver, and taking him on one side he added, 'This is Ganelon's doing—he has betrayed us.'

'How dare you accuse him!' cried Roland. 'Ganelon is my stepfather. I will listen to no slander.'

'We are greatly outnumbered, we need help,' said Oliver. 'Dear friend and companion, blow your ivory horn so that Charlemagne may hear it and turn back.'

'What, call for help and be branded a coward?' said Roland. 'My sword Durendal is all the help I need. You shall see the blade red to the hilt with pagan blood, I swear it.'

'Roland, dear friend,' said Oliver with grave courtesy, a second time. 'Blow your ivory horn so that Charlemagne may hear it and turn back.'

'I refuse to disgrace my Emperor,' said Roland. 'I shall fight. I shall lay about me right and left with Durendal. The pagans will be sorry they ever came here.'

A third time Oliver said, 'Roland, dear friend,

blow your ivory horn so that Charlemagne may hear it and turn back. He is at the Gates of Spain and will not stay.'

'People would say I was afraid of the pagans,' said Roland. 'I could not bear the shame.'

'I see no shame in it,' said Oliver, who was as brave as Roland but a wiser soldier. 'I tell you, I have seen the Saracens. The valleys are choked with them, they spill over the plains and the hills and the mountains, numberless as the waves of the sea. We have only a handful to meet them.'

'All the more chance for us to win glory,' said Roland. 'I am hungry for battle. I would rather die than bring dishonour to France.'

There was a rumble of thunder in the distance, and far away at the end of the valley a white dust rose.

'Look—the pagans are already in sight!' said Oliver, and the dust cloud grew larger. 'Do you hear the ringing hooves and the fury of their riding?' The rumble grew louder. 'They are close to us, but Charlemagne is miles away—because you are too stubborn to blow your horn. Had he been here, he could have saved us. Look up towards the Gates of Spain and see how dangerously the reservoir is placed. We're in a trap.'

'Coward!' cried Roland. 'Why don't you go home? We must stand fast and fight hard——'

'——and all be killed,' said Oliver.

'My lord companion, you must not talk like that,' said Roland, and no leopard or lion ever looked fiercer than he did. 'It is right that a man should suffer for his lord. He should endure winter snow and the scorch of summer, he should bleed for him in battle. Strike with your lance as I shall with Durendal, the sword that Charlemagne gave me. I may die, but what of that? Death is no disgrace.'

Then Archbishop Turpin of Rheims spurred his horse forward. Mounting a bare hillock, he looked down on the French host and called out, 'My lord barons, our Emperor Charlemagne has left us here and it is our duty to die for him. Stand for the Christian faith, confess your sins and pray for God's mercy. Do not be afraid to die—you will be true martyrs and dwell in Paradise.'

The French dismounted and, when they had confessed their sins, the Archbishop blessed them. And they made ready for battle.

Then Roland called Oliver to him and said, 'My lord companion, you were right about Ganelon—he did betray us. He must have done it for a bribe. But Charlemagne will have vengeance and Marsila will pay dearly for his buying.'

He spurred his swift charger—its name was Watchman—and galloped off right to the Gates of Spain. How splendid he looked in his armour! A milk-white pennon was laced to the steel of his lance, its long fringes dangling to his wrists, and he clasped it firmly, with the tip pointing high into the sky. Oh, he was handsome beyond measure, his face radiant with laughter—all sweetness to the French, but all fierceness to the foe.

'My lord barons,' he said, 'you are riding too fast. Rein in your horses. These pagans are looking for trouble—and before nightfall, by Heaven, they shall have it.'

But Oliver was in a bitter mood.

'You will have no help from Charlemagne,' he said. 'He knows nothing of our plight, but the blame is yours, not his. You were too stubborn to blow your horn.'

He turned to the French and exhorted them to ride as well as they could, to stand firm and strike hard. And he shouted their battle cry, 'Mountjoy!'

'Mountjoy!' cried the French, and they spurred their horses forward.

God, how glorious was their courage as they galloped into battle! The Saracens did not shrink from them, and with a din that made the mountains tremble the two armies clashed together.

VI

The Battle of Roncesvalles

AT THE HEAD of the pagan army rode Adelroth, King Marsila's nephew. He had been given the honour of being the first knight to do battle with Roland.

'Men of France, your Emperor Charlemagne has betrayed you and left you to die here,' he cried. 'He must be mad. But he shall pay for it before nightfall—with Roland's death.'

D

Those were the last words he ever spoke, for Roland spurred his horse and, running at him with all his strength, cut through his spine and hurled him dead from his horse.

'Charlemagne is no traitor!' he cried. 'He was right to leave us in the Pass. Men of France, we have won the first encounter. Strike hard, for God is on our side. Today our country's fame shall ring to high Heaven.'

'No, it shall be dragged in the dust, trampled under our horses' hooves,' cried Fulsaron, King Marsila's brother.

The words were hardly out of his mouth when Oliver, pricking his horse with his golden spurs, shattered Fulsaron's shield and coat of mail, thrust hard into his body and threw him dead from the saddle.

The Saracens wavered. They groaned aloud when they saw this. But Corsalis, King of Barbary, a fearless warrior steeped in villainy and the black ways of wickedness, rallied them and said, 'The French have no chance against us. They are few and feeble, and Charlemagne cannot save them.'

The Archbishop heard this and it was more than he could stomach. He charged at Corsalis with his spear and, driving it straight through his body, rolled him dead at his feet.

'Liar and slave!' he cried, as he looked down on the dead body sprawling on the grass. 'We shall do the same for all your fellows. Mountjoy!'

'Mountjoy!' shouted the French and, encouraged by the Archbishop's example, they fell upon the foe.

Foremost of them all was Roland. Hacking through the press with his spear, in fifteen blows he broke the shaft. Then he drew his sword Durendal and struck at Chernible, the cruel pagan who came from a land of devils that grew no living thing, where there was neither sun nor rain nor dew and every stone was black. Roland shattered the rubies blazing on his helmet and cut through his body deep into the horse's saddle. Chernible's huge bulk toppled to the ground, entangled in his long hair.

'Mohammed can do nothing for you now,' said Roland scornfully.

Bravely he carved his way through the Saracens, and the bright blood flowed thick on the field. His coat of mail and his arms were red, and so were his horse's neck and shoulders.

Oliver's deeds were no less valiant. After breaking the shaft of his lance, he had to use the butt, which was all that remained. With this he lunged at Malun, a pagan with a shield of extraordinary beauty whose rim framed a circle of painted flowers. What use was it against Oliver? One blow was enough to shatter it and his pagan brains as well, and Oliver flung the dead body on a heap of seven hundred slain.

Roland looked at the jagged butt.

'What are you doing with that, my lord companion?' he asked. 'A piece of stick is no good in a battle like this—you need iron and steel. Where is your sword Starbright with its gold and jewelled hilt?'

'I have had no time to draw it—I've been too busy fighting,' said Oliver, and he plucked it from his scabbard.

'Mountjoy!' cried the French as he laid about him, and many a dark pagan fell dead.

Fiercely and yet more fiercely raged the battle. Many a lance was broken, many a pennon bloodied and torn, and the pagans were slain in their hundreds and thousands. The bravest French warriors too lay dead upon the field. Never again would they see their wives or mothers or Charlemagne their

Emperor, anxiously waiting for them at the Gates of Spain.

And far away in France a great storm rose. The sky was ragged with thunder, tempestuous with hail and wind and rain, and there was a mighty earthquake. From Besançon to Wissant, from Saintes to St Michael-of-the-Seas hardly a house was left standing. Noonday was dark as night, lit only with the lightning that streaked across the sky. The wind rocked the forests and the pine trees whistled the note of doom. What misfortune did this fury foretell? Some said it was the end of the world, that doomsday had come. But they could not read the signs—they did not know that earth and Heaven were sorrowing because Roland was to die.

Valiantly the French fought on till out of a hundred thousand pagans not two were left alive.

'There has never been such a battle since the world began,' said the Archbishop.

In their triumph they did not forget their dead and wounded. They went through the field searching for them, caring for the maimed with great tenderness and weeping for lost friends and kinsmen as if their hearts would break.

Meanwhile the second pagan army was waiting, and King Marsila came riding up the valley with twenty divisions, their shields and jewelled helmets flashing in the sun. Seven thousand trumpets heralded their coming, and the huge din echoed from peak to peak.

'Oliver, my brother, my dear companion,' said
Roland. 'You were right about Ganelon—he has
sworn to have us killed. But the Emperor will
avenge our deaths. The battle will be hard, yet you
and I will fight side by side, as we have done so
many times before. Starbright will gleam in your
hand and Durendal in mine, and minstrels down
the years will sing of our shining deeds.'

When Marsila saw the wreck of his army—a
hundred thousand of his best men slaughtered—he
trembled with anger. He sent the Saracen Abisme,

the most vicious of his knights, to the front, then ordered his horns and trumpets to sound the advance.

Abisme was as black as pitch and loved treachery and murder more than all the gold in Galicia. Nobody had ever seen him laugh, and Marsila valued him only because, in spite of his dullard wits, he was brave.

The Archbishop looked scornfully at him, at the dragon on the banner he was carrying, and at the cheering mob about him.

'A true heretic,' he muttered. 'He would be better dead. As I have the honour to begin the fight, I shall start with him.'

He patted his horse, a splendid creature he had taken from a king he had once killed in Denmark. It was swift and spirited, long in the flank, high-backed, with slender legs, short thighs and firm haunches. The tail was white, the mane yellow, and it had small ears and a tawny face—a perfect horse for battle.

The Archbishop spurred his steed straight at Abisme, pointing his lance straight at the dazzling jewels, the topaz and the amethyst that blazed upon his shield. He split the shield as if it were matchwood, and cut clean through his body from side to side, then flung it to the ground.

'A good soldier, and a good Christian too!' cried the French, and they cheered him to the echo.

Turpin galloped back to the line. 'Stand your ground!' he cried. 'It is better to die fighting than to flee. Soon we shall be killed, and not one of us will live to see the rising of the sun. But this I promise —the Gates of Paradise are open wide to you, and you shall dwell with the Innocents for ever.'

'Mountjoy!' cried the French, and they took heart from his words.

The first Frenchman to fall was Count Engelier of Gascony. He was killed by Climborin, a pagan from Saragossa who had received the oath from Ganelon and kissed the traitor in friendship. But Oliver was quick to take his revenge. He rode at him full tilt, and a single blow from Starbright struck him down dead. And Satan carried off his sinful soul to hell.

Climborin was the first of many pagans to fall to Oliver's sword. He beheaded Escababa and unhorsed seven Arabs. These Arabs were brave men, and their horses were faster than falcons, swifter than hawks or swallows. But none of them could stand up to Oliver.

Roland was fully as brave as he. He avenged Duke Sanson's death by killing Valdabron, master of four hundred ships and spoiler of Jerusalem. Even Prince Grandonie of Cappadocia, who had slain many of the noblest knights of France, quailed before Roland. Though the Prince did all he could to dodge him, Roland sought him out and came upon him suddenly in the thick of battle.

The Prince had never met him before, but who could fail to recognize Roland's handsome looks and proud bearing? The colour fled from his cheeks and he panicked like a netted bird.

'You shall pay dearly for your butchery and for the grief you have brought to us,' said Roland. Before the Prince had time to escape, he struck him with Durendal. The blow cut through his helmet, right through his body and his coat of mail and deep into the horse's back, killing both rider and horse.

'A magnificent blow,' said the French.

But the Saracens yelled with dismay.

Fiercely and yet more fiercely raged the battle. French swords flashed like lightning, hacking through wrists and ribs and backs; French lances cut through coats of mail to the living flesh till the blood ran red on the grass. Men were hurled from their horses, sucked into the surge of battle, like trees uprooted in the spring floods, and whirled away. Bodies lay everywhere sprawled in heaps, on their faces and their backs, the wounded and the dead together.

The pagans could stand no more.

'Ride, ride, Marsila!' they cried. 'Help us in our agony!'

But the French clung on. With the last of their strength they chased the pagans from the field.

VII

The Sounding of the Horn

THE FRENCH TRIUMPHED in three encounters, but the fourth was a disaster and all but sixty of their knights were slain. As Roland looked round about him, there was no sadder man in the world than he. The flower of French knighthood lay dead on the field.

'Dear Oliver, in God's Name what are we to do?' he said. 'We cannot hold back the pagans without Charlemagne. Why is he not here? Is there no way of sending him news?'

'How should I know?' said Oliver.

'I can sound my horn. He is at the Gates of Spain and will hear it and turn back.'

'That would be a shameful thing to do. Your kinsmen would never live it down.'

'Why shameful?' said Roland.

'Because there are only ourselves to save now. If you blow it, I shall have nothing to do with you.'

'I shall call Charlemagne, whatever you may think.'

'Coward!'

'I have fought hard all day.'

'I can see the blood on your arms,' said Oliver. 'But I still call you a coward. If you had listened to me before, Charlemagne could have saved the whole rearguard and Marsila would have been captured or killed. It is too late now.' Still smouldering with resentment, he added, 'If ever I set eyes on Alda again, I'll see that she loves you no more.'

Alda was Oliver's sister, betrothed to Roland, and she loved him with all her heart.

Roland was silent for a moment. Then he said, 'Oliver, why are you so angry with me?'

'Because you are to blame for all our troubles. Will you never learn that a little wisdom is better than all your monstrous arrogance? Why are our men all dead? Why will they never serve their Emperor again? Because of your bungling. And before evening you will be as dead as they are.'

'We have been friends for so long. Must we part in bitterness?' said Roland.

Just then the Archbishop came galloping up.

'Lord Oliver—Lord Roland—in God's Name stop quarrelling,' he said.

'Roland wants to sound his horn,' said Oliver. 'As if that could help us now!'

'Of course it cannot help,' said the Archbishop.

'Then forbid him to do it.'

'No,' said the Archbishop. 'It is right to call Charlemagne. He will avenge us and prevent the Saracens from escaping. For ourselves he can do nothing, for we shall be dead and torn to pieces. But our countrymen will search for our bodies and weep for us. No wolf or hound or wild boar will feed on our flesh, for we shall be laid in coffins and carried home and buried in the minster-close.'

'Good advice,' said Roland. 'I shall do as you say.'

He set the ivory horn to his lips and blew it with all his dwindling strength. And the sound of it went ringing high over the valleys and the mountains, echoing from peak to peak.

Thirty leagues away Charlemagne heard it, and he halted in his march.

'Listen! Our men are fighting,' he said.

'They are not,' said Ganelon. 'Sir, I will not call you a liar, but if anyone but you had said that——'

'Listen!' said the Emperor.

Again, and in great anguish, Roland blew his horn. He burst the veins of his temple and blood spurted from his mouth. And the sound of the horn went ringing high over the valleys and the mountains, echoing from peak to peak.

Charlemagne heard it as he rode through the Pass. Ganelon and all the Frenchmen heard it.

'That was Roland's horn,' said the Emperor. 'He would never have sounded it if he were not fighting.'

'I tell you, there is no battle,' said Ganelon. 'You are growing old, your hair is white and withered, and you talk like a child. You know how stubborn Roland is—it amazes me that God has let him live so long. When he took Naples, you remember, it was against your orders. He didn't want you to find out, so what did he do? He swilled down the battle-field to wash away the blood.'

'Roland is calling for help,' said the Emperor.

'No, sir, he is showing off in front of his men,' said Ganelon. 'When he is out hunting he will blow his horn from dawn to dusk for one wretched hare. He would never call for help—he is too proud for that.'

'The pagans are attacking him,' said the Emperor.

'No one in the world would be so rash,' said Ganelon. 'Why are you lingering here? Ride on, sir —we have a long way to go.'

The blood was gushing from Roland's mouth, draining his strength away. Once again, in dreadful anguish, he blew his horn. Faintly over the valleys and the mountains it sounded, echoing from peak to peak.

Charlemagne heard it. Duke Naimon heard it.

'That was a long blast,' said the Emperor.

'It was a cry of despair,' said the Duke.

'And Ganelon tries to tell me there is no battle,' said Charlemagne.

'Of course there is a battle, and the man who denies it is Roland's betrayer,' said the Duke. 'To arms, then! Let our battle cry ring to Heaven! Roland is calling us and we must speed to his help.'

'Sound the trumpets, answer his call!' said the Emperor. 'We shall turn back.'

And all the trumpets sounded.

In nervous haste the French put on their armour, their helmets and their coats of mail, and buckled to their sides their golden swords. In the bright evening light the sun's flame danced on their helmets, and the flowers sparkled on their painted shields. But they were trembling with fear for Roland, muttering to each other through their tears, 'God grant that we reach him in time! May we yet fight at his side and keep him from death!'

What use were their words? They had waited too long.

And they mounted their horses and spurred through the sun and shadow of the Pass, the pennons on their lance-tips streaming in the wind— purple, emerald and flaming gold.

Meanwhile the Emperor had arrested Ganelon and given him over to the cooks in his field-kitchen. He called Besgun, his master-cook, to him and said, 'Guard him closely—he is a traitor. He has betrayed me and all my house.'

So Besgun took Ganelon in charge. A hundred kitchen knaves sprang upon him, plucking his beard

and moustache, punching him in the face and beating him with sticks and cudgels. They put a chain
round his neck as if he were a bear and hoisted him,
smarting with shame, on to a pack-horse. And they
watched him eagle-eyed, ready to pounce if he
stirred an inch.

'Sound the trumpets again!' said the Emperor.
'Roland must know for sure that we are coming!'

All the trumpets sounded, echoing from peak to
peak.

Charlemagne rode on, his white beard blowing
on his breastplate, his eyes wild with anger.

And his huge army rode
on—through the dark and
winding valleys, in the shadow of the mountains, past
rivers that tumbled over
rock and boulder racing for
the distant sea.

And Roland and his sixty
knights, battle-scarred, bowed down with weariness and
very near to death, fought
on and refused to yield.

E

VIII

The Death of Oliver

ROLAND LOOKED OUT over the valley and
the hills where the multitude of French lay
dead.

'My lord barons,' he said, 'you have served me
long and loyally and won great victories for your
Emperor—and I have brought you to this sad ending. I have robbed my country of her noblest sons.'
He paused and for some moments could not speak
for grief. 'I leave you to God's mercy, for I can do no

more. May He bring your souls to the Gates of Light. May you lie down in the flowered fields of Heaven and find rest. . . . Oliver, my friend and companion, let us go back and fight.'

So Roland returned to the field. Laying about him mightily with Durendal, he slew twenty-five of the bravest pagans. Those that were left scattered before him like frightened deer in the chase.

'I love to see bravery like yours,' said Turpin. 'You sit your horse proudly and bear your arms without flinching, terrible as a lion in battle. That is the pattern of true knighthood. Anyone here who cannot live up to it had better turn monk and go on his knees and pray for our souls instead.'

'There are only true knights among us here,' said Roland, and he galloped after the pagans.

The French took heart from his example and returned to the fray. Though they were going to their deaths, they fought like lions. Almost at once they met King Marsila, spurring hard towards them, and four of them died on the point of his steel.

'God rot your soul!' cried Roland, when he saw the smirk of triumph on Marsila's face. 'You have killed my friends and now, by Heaven, you shall taste my steel!' And he struck off King Marsila's right hand, then with a second blow the head of Jurfaret his son.

The pagans trembled and turned pale with terror. 'Help us, Mohammed!' they cried. 'Give us vengeance against Charlemagne. These men he has sent against us are not human—they face certain death and still they will not run.'

It was the pagans who ran, a hundred thousand of them, with King Marsila at their head. Call them back, go on calling till the mountains fall about your ears—they will not return.

But the Caliph, the King's uncle, stayed behind. He was master of Ethiopia, country of the damned, and he had fifty thousand of his followers at his heel. With their big noses and broad ears they were black as pitch from head to toe and only their smiles were white. They looked scornfully at the pitiful remains of the rearguard, then rode like thunder against them, shouting their fiendish battle cry as they went.

'There is no hope for us now,' said Roland when he saw them. 'We shall die, but we shall all be martyrs for the Faith. Sell your lives dearly—we cannot disgrace our country. When Charlemagne comes, he will find fifteen dead Saracens for every one of us and he will bless us for our deeds. Fight on!'

'And show no mercy!' said Oliver.

The French returned to the attack.

Then the Caliph did a treacherous and unknightly deed. Spurring his sorrel horse, he whirled round and charged at Oliver from behind. He drove his spear through the middle of his back, breaking his coat of mail and thrusting the point right through his chest.

'Charlemagne will relish this!' he cried. 'One blow of mine has settled all our losses.'

Though he knew he had received his death wound, Oliver still had some strength left. He raised Starbright, his sword of shining steel, high above his head, then brought it crashing down on to the Caliph's golden helmet, splintering the flowers and the crystal gems and cutting clean through his skull.

'May your soul be damned!' said Oliver. 'You thought you would return home to boast of your prowess. Now you never will. Your Spanish ladies will wait for you in vain.'

He launched into the fight again, hacking through the jungle of spears and shields, through hands and feet and saddles and sides. As he threw the bodies in heaps about him, he shouted 'Mountjoy!' at the top of his voice.

At last he was exhausted and called to Roland to come and help him.

Roland was amazed by his courage, but when he saw his companion's face he was moved to his very soul. It was livid and ghastly, and blood was gushing from his wounds. Oliver was dying. Charlemagne would mourn him, France would be desolate without him. But what could Roland do for him now? Overcome by the sight of such suffering, he swooned in the saddle, swaying unsteadily from side to side. Only the long stirrups prevented him from falling.

Oliver had lost so much blood that his eyes were blurred and misty and he could no longer recognize anybody, not even Roland. He urged his horse forward a few paces to where his companion was, then grasped his sword-hilt with both hands and brought the blade crashing down on to Roland's helmet. It cut through the jewelled plating as far as the nose-piece, but did not harm his head.

Dazed and reeling from the blow, Roland looked

up and asked him gently, 'Oliver, did you mean to strike me? I am Roland—I have loved you all my life.'

'I know your voice,' said Oliver, 'but I cannot see you clearly.'

'Are you still angry with me? Is that why you struck me? You never challenged me.'

'God keep you, Roland. I did not mean to strike you.'

'I am not hurt.'

'Forgive me, dear friend,' said Oliver.

'I forgive you in God's Name.'

With grave courtesy they bowed to each other, and then parted—not in anger or distress of mind, but in love.

Oliver felt the pangs of death coming upon him. His eyes were swimming in his head, and he could neither see nor hear. Slowly and painfully dismounting, he knelt and confessed his sins aloud. He lifted his clasped hands to Heaven and prayed to

God to give him rest in Paradise, to bless Charlemagne and France and his companion Roland
above all men. Then his head sank on his breast,
his body slumped forward, and he lay on his face
full length on the ground. So Oliver died, and his
soul vanished from the world of men.

For a while Roland watched over him, weeping
and mourning for him—there was no sadder man
on earth—and gently calling his name.

'My lord and companion, through long days and
years you and I have been closer than brothers,
sharing together the storm and the rain and the
sunlight. In all that time we have never been false
to each other. Now you are dead, I have no will
to go on living.'

A great wave of grief swallowed him, so that he
swooned in the saddle, swaying unsteadily. Only
the long stirrups prevented him from falling.

And there was a great stillness on the battle-field,
as if all living things had perished.

IX

Archbishop Turpin

WHEN ROLAND CAME to his senses, he saw all round him nothing but the bodies of the slain. Of the rearguard all but two were dead—Count Walter and the Archbishop. Count Walter had been up on the heights fighting the Saracens and had lost his whole company. His nerve shaken, he came galloping down into the valley looking for Roland and shouting to him for help.

'Gentle count, brave soldier, where are you?' he

cried. 'I was never afraid when you were near me.
. . . I am Walter, your old comrade in arms—you
used to praise me for my valour. And now my lance
is broken, my shield split, my coat of mail ripped
to pieces, and I am dying. But I have made the
pagans pay for all they have done. Roland, where
are you?'

Roland heard him and galloped over to help,
taking the Archbishop with him. Farther up the
valley he could see the Saracens rallying for another
attack. Wild with grief and anger, he rode to meet
them, with Count Walter and the Archbishop on
either side. Soon he had overthrown twenty, while
Walter had slain six and the Archbishop five.

'These men tear us like wolves,' said the pagans.
'We must kill them quickly before they savage us
again.'

With a great yell they burst upon them from all
sides at once—a thousand foot-soldiers, forty thousand cavalry—all against three men. But where in
all the world would you find three men like them?
The pagans did not dare go near them.

Standing well out of range they let loose a hail-
storm of lances and spears and darts and javelins.
In the first attack they killed Count Walter and
pierced the Archbishop through the chest with four
spears, as well as wounding him in the head. The
Archbishop's helmet was smashed, his mailcoat torn,
and his horse killed under him. Grievously wounded
though he was, he leaped up lightly and ran to
Roland and said, 'I am not beaten yet. I shall
fight as long as I have breath in me.'

He drew his sword of shining steel and struck a thousand blows in the thickest of the battle. Afterwards Charlemagne was to find four hundred pagans lying round him, some wounded, some transfixed with spears, and some beheaded.

And Roland fought on. His body was streaming with sweat, and his head was on fire from the pain of his burst temple. Was Charlemagne never coming? Once again he put his horn to his lips and blew it with the last of his dwindling strength.

Over the mountains and the valleys it sounded, ringing faintly from peak to peak, and the last echo was like the whisper of a dying man.

Twenty leagues away the Emperor heard it, and he halted in his march.

'My lord barons,' he said, 'the pagans have beaten us. My nephew Roland is dying—I can tell it from the sound of his horn. If you are to reach him in time you must ride like the mountain wind. Blow the trumpets again—with all your might.'

All the trumpets sounded, sixty thousand of them in one piercing blast. And the noise went ringing high over the valleys and the mountains, echoing from peak to peak.

The pagans heard it—and it dashed the laughter from their lips. They turned pale with terror.

'Listen!' they cried. 'The French are coming back in their thousands and tens of thousands. If Roland is still alive when Charlemagne comes, there will be more slaughter and our country will be lost. We must kill him at once.'

Four hundred of their finest warriors, banded

together in tight phalanx, their shields levelled and their lances poised, bore down on Roland in one terrific onslaught. Their horseshoes rang on the baked earth; they trampled the brown grasses, raising clouds of dust as they went.

Roland did not wait for them but pricked his golden spurs into Watchman's flanks and rode to meet them. And the brave Archbishop, grievously wounded, ran beside him, gasping for breath.

Soon, in pity for his friend, Roland stopped. He could not leave him to lag behind.

'Let us stand together here and face the enemy,' he said. 'Durendal shall carve out a way for us both.'

As he spoke, far away in the distance the French trumpets sounded, and the faint cry of 'Mountjoy!' trembled over the hills.

'The Emperor is coming—he will soon be here—he will avenge us,' gasped the Archbishop.

The pagans wavered in mid-field, and a great fear swept through their ranks like wind in the ripening corn.

'Doom and disaster!' they cried. 'The trumpets are sounding Charlemagne's return—his hordes are upon us!'

They paused in confusion, their horses champing and rearing, and glared angrily at Roland. He was waiting patiently for them beside the Archbishop, unmoved by their multitude, firm as a rock.

'There's no man in the world who can put Roland down,' they cried. 'Let us hurl our spears at him and run!'

They hurled them—and the sky was darkened

with a whining storm of spears and lances and javelins and feathered darts. His shield was cracked and broken, his coat of mail smashed, and Watchman—gashed in thirty places—killed under him. But Roland himself was untouched.

The pagans did not linger. Wild and angry as the raging sea, they fled towards Spain.

Without his horse Roland could not give chase. So he went over to help the Archbishop. Unlacing his helmet and stripping off his coat of mail, he cut his friend's shirt into strips and used them to bandage his wounds. Then he lifted him up, holding him close to his breast, and lowered him to the grass as gently as if he had been a sick child.

'Noble sir, may I leave you for a while?' said Roland, very softly. 'There is one last service I must do for our friends. Though they are all dead now, we loved them dearly, and it would be wrong to let them lie where they fell. I will go and look for them and bring them together here for you to see.'

'Of course you may go,' said the Archbishop. 'But come back to me, Roland. This is our field—yours and mine—God gave us victory here.'

Roland turned away and began his lonely search through the valleys and along the slopes of the hills for his dead friends. He found nine of the Twelve Peers and, carrying them one by one to the Archbishop, laid them down in front of him. With tears in his eyes, the Archbishop raised his hand to bless them.

'May your souls find rest in the flowered fields of Paradise,' he said. 'Like you, I shall not see my

Emperor again, for I am torn with pain and very near to death.'

There was still one Peer whom Roland had not found—Oliver, his companion—so he went back to look for him. In a little while he returned, clasping him to his breast, very careful not to slip or stumble. He laid him on a shield beside the others, and the Archbishop absolved and blessed them all.

'Oliver, my dear companion,' said Roland, in a voice choked with sorrow, 'you were a great soldier. No one could break a lance or split a shield like you, no one could humble the proud or cheer the brave with winning words as you did—no one in the world.'

The colour drained from his cheeks. Spent with grief and exhaustion, he fell to the ground.

In deep concern for him, the Archbishop reached out his hand for Roland's horn and grasped it. He wanted to fill it with water to revive him, for there was a mountain stream close by, tumbling over rock and boulder down-valley toward the distant sea. He gasped for breath, he heaved himself to his feet and staggered a few faltering steps. But he was faint for loss of blood and very weak, and before he had gone fifty paces he stumbled. Falling on his face, with a cry of anguish he died.

When Roland came to his senses, dazed with the pain in his head, he struggled to his feet. Where was the Archbishop? He looked along the valley and up to the hills—then caught sight of him lying on the grass beyond his companions, not far from the stream. He was lying in a pool of blood, his hand outstretched towards the water, clasping the horn.

So Turpin was dead, noble Turpin, sworn enemy of all pagans, on the battle-field and in the pulpit the fearless champion of the Faith.

Roland knelt down by the body and lifted his eyes and hands in prayer to high Heaven.

'Gentle knight, loyal servant of Christ,' he said, 'I commend you now to the heavenly saints. Since the days of the Apostles there has been no minister of God's law, no leader of men to match you. May your soul be cleansed of suffering, may it wing its way to the Gates of Light.'

He was silent, and there was no sound at all save the murmur of the water. Then he took the Archbishop's hands in his own—they were white and beautiful as April flowers—and crossed them on his breast.

X

The Death of Roland

ROLAND'S BRAIN SEEMED to be bursting in
his head. He knew he had not long to live.
In one hand he held Durendal, in the other
his ivory horn, which he had taken from Turpin's
fingers. With a prayer to the angel Gabriel to give
him strength, he began to walk through the battle-
wasted fields towards Spain.

When he had gone some little way—about the
length of an arrow's flight—he came to a hill with

four boundary stones of gleaming marble standing in the shadow of a pine tree. He climbed as far as the stones, but the effort was too much for him and he fell fainting on the grass. Above him rose the tree, above the tree the white peaks of the mountains, above the mountains the burning sky. And Roland lay there in the coolness, very near to death.

All this time a Saracen had been hiding in a heap of bodies at the foot of the hill, watching him. He had smeared his face and body all over with blood and was pretending to be dead. As soon as Roland fell, he jumped up and ran up the hill—he was power- fully built and fleet-footed as the mountain wind. Thinking that Roland was finished, he threw himself upon him. 'I'll have his sword and wear it in Arabia,' he cried, and reached out with his greedy hand. But at the touch of his fingers, Roland opened his eyes.

'Who are you? Not one of us,' said Roland.

He lifted his ivory horn and brought it crashing down on to the Saracen's helmet, breaking through the steel and the skull together. 'You were mad to try a trick like that on me!' he cried, as he threw the body to the ground.

He reached down for his horn—then started back in horror.

'Pagan cur, you have smashed the mouth of my horn!'

He stooped to pick up the gold and crystal frag- ments from the ground, but his eyes were misty with death and he could not see clearly. The colour had gone from his face, and it was all he could do to stagger to his feet.

'I still have my sword,' he said. 'No one shall have that.'

In front of him he could dimly see a dark rock, which was firm and hard to the touch. Summoning the little remnant of his strength, he struck the rock ten times with his sword. The steel grated but would not crack or splinter.

'I am Durendal's keeper and was mighty once, but I am all weakness now,' he said. 'Blessed St Mary, fill me with strength.'

He struck yet another blow, and again the steel grated but would not crack or splinter.

'Durendal, my shining sword,' he said, 'you have lost none of your splendour. Your lightning still flashes in the sun. You came to me in far-off days, the gift of Charlemagne, at the bidding of God's angel. Since then what victories have been ours, what countries have we won from Lombardy to Scotland, from Bavaria to Spain—and all for the glory of Charlemagne, for the might and majesty of his throne! How could I let you fall into pagan hands?'

He struck until the rock was shattered. At the final blow his sword rebounded upward to the sky, but still it would not crack or splinter.

When Roland saw that he had no hope of breaking it, he began to lament softly to himself: 'Durendal, my shining sword, your hilt is set with holy relics—St Peter's tooth, a drop of St Basil's blood, some hairs of St Denis, and a piece of St Mary's robe—how precious and sacred you are! It would be sacrilege for pagans to possess you. Only Christians should serve you.'

He lay down on the cool grass, with his sword and the broken horn under his body. Death was very near—he could feel it stealing fast from his head down to his heart. Before it claimed him, he was careful to turn towards Spain. He wanted Charlemagne to see that he had died with his face to the foe, like a conqueror.

As he lay there, he thought of many things—of the countries his had overthrown, of France his fatherland, of his kinsmen, and above all of Charlemagne his lord and Emperor who had brought him up from childhood in his own household—and he could not hold back his tears. He remembered also the sins of his life, the great ones and the small ones. And lifting his right glove to Heaven in atonement for them, he beat his breast and begged God's forgiveness.

'Father of all Truth,' he prayed, 'who raised up Lazarus from the dead and guarded Daniel from the lions, save my soul from all the dangers to which my sins have brought it.'

His head sank on his arm and, with his hands still clasped in prayer, he died.

From Paradise God sent St Gabriel and with him St Michael-of-the-Seas; and they flew between the white peaks down to Roncesvalles and spread over Roland their gentle wings. St Michael took his glove and St Gabriel his soul, and together they carried them to Paradise, up through the blue regions to the Gates of Light.

XI

The Return of Charlemagne

SO ROLAND DIED and his soul found rest in
Paradise.

The Emperor rode on to Roncesvalles and,
looking out upon the battle-field, saw the measure of his ruin. Christians and pagans were lying
everywhere—on the grass, on the bare rocks, between the roots of wild flowers—the ground was
thick with the bodies of the slain.

'Roland, my nephew, where are you?' he shouted. 'Where is the Archbishop, and Oliver? Where are the rest of my Twelve Peers?' And he called them each by name.

But what was the use of calling? They were gone where no voice could call them back.

'God!' he cried. 'If only I had been there when the fighting started!' Bitter with self-reproach, he plucked wildly at his beard.

Every baron there had lost someone dear to him, a son or brother, nephew, friend or liege-lord, and they mourned and grieved for them as if their hearts would break.

Duke Naimon was the first to speak. He pointed to a cloud two leagues away and said, 'Look, the roads are smoking with a great dust whirled up by hoof and heel—the pagans are running for their lives. Ride, sir, and avenge this disaster.'

'We cannot catch them—they have already gone too far,' said Charlemagne. And in his agony he cried, 'They have robbed me of my rearguard, all my sons of valour and delight!'

But when he reflected on the Duke's counsel, he thought it sound and honourable. Summoning four of his counts, he commanded them, 'Stay here and watch the fields, the hills and the valleys. Leave the dead to lie where they are. But you must guard them from lions and all prowling beasts, and see that nobody goes near them till we return.'

Lovingly and reverently the counts answered, 'Dear lord and Emperor, we shall obey you.'

And they stayed behind, keeping a thousand knights with them.

The trumpets sounded the advance. The whole army, with the Emperor at their head, spurred their horses forward, in hot pursuit of the pagans. But when he saw how late it was and that the fires of the sunset were burning low, he dismounted and, kneeling down in a meadow, prayed to God to hold back the coming of the dark.

He opened his eyes and an angel was there beside him.

'Ride, ride, Charlemagne,' he said. 'You have lost the flower of France, your sons of valour and delight, God knows that well. But the light will not fail you. There is still time to take your vengeance.'

Then God did a great miracle for Charlemagne. He took the sun and fixed it in the firmament, rooted, motionless. And the pagans fled before the French like deer in the chase, onward and ever onward. In the Valley of Darkness the Christians caught them and fell upon them, cutting them to pieces as they ran, blocking every track and by-way so they could not escape—till they drove them against the banks of the River Ebro. Deep and tumultuous with headlong racing waters, this was a barrier the pagans could not pass. They looked to right and to left—there was no boat or barge to be seen. Terrified they plunged in, calling upon their god Termagant to save them. But what did he care? He let them all drown, some weighed down by their armour, some whirled away on the flood of waters. Lucky were those who sank and died quickly.

So the pagans all perished, most of them by drowning, though a number had been killed on the river bank or in the rout beforehand. All that was left of them was a few scattered bodies, which the French knights soon stripped of plunder.

Charlemagne dismounted and knelt down on the grass to give thanks to God. When he opened his eyes and rose to his feet, the sun had vanished. It was night and the stars were shining.

'We must camp here,' he said. 'It is too late to return to Roncesvalles and our horses are worn out. Unsaddle them, take off their bridles, let them graze in the meadows.'

The French dismounted and let their horses loose. Poor beasts, they were so exhausted that they could not stand upright. If they wanted grass, they cropped it lying down. The French too were exhausted.

Without troubling to post any sentinels, they lay down on the ground and fell asleep at once.

The Emperor lay down beside his soldiers. He was still wearing his white coat of mail with its purple border; his great spear was at his head and his sword at his side. And what a sword it was—there was none like it in all the world. The blade was made from the lance-head that had wounded Christ on the cross, and Charlemagne had had it set in a golden hilt. He was so proud of the sword that he called it Joyous.

And the moon rose high above the sleeping hills, filling the valleys with light, cleansing them of slaughter.

But Charlemagne could not sleep. He was sick with grief for Roland and Oliver, for the rest of the Twelve Peers, for all the French lying dead on the field; and the burden of their dying was terrible to bear. As he prayed to God to watch over their souls, he could not hold back his tears. At last he lay back, utterly weary, and soon he was heavily asleep like the soldiers in the fields all round him.

Then God sent St Gabriel to stand all night at his head and watch over him while he slept. And the angel showed him in a dream signs of a great battle to come. Charlemagne looked up and saw the sky tempestuous with wind and hail and thunder. Tongues of fire shot down from the storm-clouds to feast upon his people, consuming their spears of ashwood, shrivelling their shields right to the golden bosses, melting sword and helmet and coat of mail in the fierce heat. Bears and leopards pounced upon his barons eager to devour them, snakes and vipers too, dragons and black devils. In their agony the French cried out, 'Help us, Charlemagne!' He ran to them, but a lion rose out of a wood, barring his road, and sprang upon him. Man and beast grappled and fought together, rocking this way and that in mortal combat, and there was no telling which would win. . . . And Charlemagne slept on without waking.

Soon his sleep was troubled with another dream. He was at Aix leading a bear on a double chain, when suddenly from the forest of Ardennes there appeared thirty more bears. 'Sir, give him back to us,' they said, speaking with the voices of men. 'You have no right to him—he is ours.' Then a greyhound bounded out of the Emperor's palace. Choosing the biggest of the bears, he leapt at him and struggled with him on the grass beyond his fellows. Long and furiously they fought, but there was no telling which would win.

All these things St Gabriel showed to Charlemagne. And he slept on without waking—till dawn, till the first light roused him and the warmth of day crept back into the hills.

XII

The Emir Baligant

A SOLITARY HORSEMAN, in headlong flight from the French army, was galloping over the plain towards Saragossa. The city on its rugged mountain of rock rose out of the distance to meet him; the gates flew open, then closed behind him. In the shade of an olive tree he drew rein and wearily dismounted. While his horse, breathless from the long journey, its mane flecked with foam, was led away, he threw down his sword and helmet and stripped off his coat of mail. As the iron rings grazed his right arm he winced with pain, for the hand had been cut off, and he slumped forward on to the grass in a faint.

It was King Marsila.

From the city ramparts Queen Bramimunde had watched him coming and as soon as she recognized him hurried down to meet him. When she saw how badly wounded he was, in great distress she threw herself at his feet. The Saracens crowded round her—twenty thousand and more—all shouting curses and insults on Charlemagne. Then off they ran to a shrine where a statue of their god Apollyon was kept.

'Traitor!' they screamed, and rushed at it and spat in its face. 'What made you betray us? Why did you bring disaster to our King? Marsila has served you well, and look how you reward him.'

They seized Apollyon's sceptre, they knocked off his crown, they tied him to a column and beat him with sticks and cudgels; then tossed him on to the ground and trampled on him. Termagant, another of their gods, had the jewel ripped out of his head-dress, and they hurled Mohammed into a ditch and left him there for pigs and dogs to foul.

In the cool shade of the olive tree King Marsila soon revived. He asked to be carried to his room. It was a beautiful room in the highest part of the palace, with a vaulted ceiling and bright colours and inscriptions on the walls. Queen Bramimunde followed him up the long staircase, weeping and lamenting and tearing her hair.

'Saragossa, city of despair,' she cried, 'what will
you do without your King? Our gods have humbled
him, they have wronged him cruelly. Long months ago
we sent to Babylon to the Emir Baligant for help. Will
he never come? Charlemagne is an old dodderer now.
He squanders his soldiers recklessly and thrives on
the smell of blood. Will no one rid us of him?'

She did not know that the Emir Baligant, after
innumerable delays, was already on his way. He
had gathered in his people from forty kingdoms
and on the first day of summer launched a fleet at
Alexandria, headed for Spain. This armada of
galleys, sailing barges and ships of war, was so huge
that it stretched right across the water as far as the
horizon, filling the lonely seas.

It was night when they reached the mouth of the
Ebro, the river in whose upper reaches so many of
King Marsila's soldiers had perished. Off-shore,
beyond the surf-line, the first ships dropped anchor
and waited for the slower galleys and barges to
arrive. Then the whole fleet sailed upstream, the
lanterns and jewels at their mastheads twinkling in
the darkness like stars. By daybreak they had left
the coast far behind them. Soon the sun was flashing
on their bright-blazoned sails and sweeping oars.
On and on up the twisting river they sped till at
last they came in sight of Saragossa on its crown of
rock. And they dropped anchor and set up camp
on the river bank.

The sun was high in heaven when the Emir left
his barge and stepped ashore. He was very old,
tough and wrinkled like a yew tree, and no living

man could remember when he was born. A carpet of white silk had been spread out for him under a laurel tree, with an ivory throne in the middle. Here he took his seat, with seventeen kings behind him and a huge company of counts and dukes standing in the field in front.

'My lords, my brave knights,' he said, surveying them proudly, 'for years the Emperor Charlemagne has been destroying us in Spain. He has gone home now, but he is sure to return. We must not let him return—no, not for all the gold under Heaven. We must seek him out in France. I will not rest till he is dead or cringing for mercy at my feet.' And he struck his knee with his right glove.

Then he called two of his knights, Clarifan and Clarien.

'Go to Saragossa,' he commanded. 'Tell King Marsila that I have come to help him against Charlemagne. I am going to France to find him —as far as Aix where he holds his court. To prove that I have sent you, take my glove, Clarifan, and see that Marsila puts it on. Clarien, take my gold rod. When you give it to him, tell him to come here and acknowledge me as his liege-lord. It was I who gave him Spain for his kingdom. To horse, then, and no lingering on the way.'

The two knights mounted their horses and rode off to Saragossa. Over four bridges, through ten gateways they galloped, and in the crowded streets of the city the pagans scattered out of their way. At last they came to the palace. There was a huge mob outside, weeping and cursing their gods.

'We have lost our King!' they cried. 'Yesterday Roland struck off his hand. And Jurfaret of the flaxen hair, we have lost him too. Our lovely land is vanquished!'

The two knights dismounted, and a Saracen took their horses by the rein and led them away. Nervously holding on to each other's cloaks, they climbed the long staircase which led to the King's room. The door was open and they went inside.

After the harsh sunlight and the hubbub outside, the room was cool and quiet. Nobody in the group round King Marsila's couch made any move to welcome them. They felt uneasier than ever.

'Greeting to you, sir,' said Clarifan, 'in the name of Mohammed and Termagant and Apollyon, the gods whom we worship.'

'May they watch over you, sir, and show favour to your Queen,' said Clarien.

Their words echoed away under the high vaulted roof. The silence was hard and cold as marble.

Suddenly Queen Bramimunde spoke. She pointed to the King, lying desperately pale on his couch.

'Fools!' she cried. 'Have you no eyes, no ears? Can you not see what these gods of ours have done to the King? Have you not heard how they failed us at Roncesvalles?' Her eyes, as she looked at the two knights, were fiery with anger and contempt. 'Charlemagne has the whole of Spain under his heel. How can we trust our gods any more? Oh, I wish I were dead!'

'You talk wildly,' said Clarien. 'The Emir Baligant has come to help King Marsila—we are

his messengers. To prove his good faith, he sends
you his rod and glove. His fleet is at anchor in the
river below—galleys and barges and ships of war,
more than four thousand of them. He has everything
you need. He intends to kill Charlemagne or make
him grovel for his life—and he will go all the way
to France to find him.'

'He can spare himself the journey,' said the Queen
bitterly. 'The Emperor is in Spain. He has already
been here seven years, and no power on earth can
drive him out. Do you really think that Baligant
can frighten him?'

Then King Marsila began to speak, so softly and
haltingly that the two messengers had to strain to
hear him.

'Leave this to me,' he said, and the words dragged
heavily and painfully from his lips. 'You can see I
am dying. I have no son or heir to succeed me—
my son Jurfaret was alive yesterday, but now he is
dead. Tell my Lord the Emir that he may come
and see me if he wishes. Here are the keys of the
city—take them to him. Tell him that I will gladly
give him back his kingdom—if only he will defend
it against Charlemagne and drive the French out.'
He paused for breath, then went on again, his voice
trembling with passion. 'Charlemagne has killed
my people, ravaged my land, destroyed my cities.
. . . Last night he was camping on the banks of the
Ebro, seven leagues from the city. Tell the Emir to
go and fight him there.'

He sank back exhausted on to his pillow.

The two knights bowed low, then called for their

horses and, much perturbed, hurried back to the Emir.

'What has happened?' asked the Emir, as Clarien handed him the keys of Saragossa. 'Where is King Marsila? I told you to send him to me.'

'He is dying,' said Clarien. 'He begs you to help him. He is ready to give you back the kingdom of Spain.'

'What news of Charlemagne?'

'Yesterday he was at the Gates of Spain on his way back to France.' And he told the Emir of how Charlemagne, after the disaster of Roncesvalles, had returned to Spain to take vengeance on the pagans, and killed them all.

The Emir hung his head in shame. He clutched the arms of his ivory throne and a great gust of anger shook him.

'Sir, there is hope for us still,' said Clarien. 'The French are not far from here. They are camping upstream on the river bank and know nothing of our arrival. We can surprise them and stop them escaping.'

To the Emir these words were like a shaft of sunlight through prison bars. His gloom vanished. He rose from his throne and looked down at the huge company of knights and dukes in the field before him, then beyond them at the ships anchored in the river.

'My lord barons, we have no time to lose,' he shouted. 'Come out of your ships, leap on your horses and ride. We can stop Charlemagne escaping and avenge King Marsila. I will give him the Emperor's head for the right hand he lost yesterday.'

The pagans poured out of their ships, leapt on to their horses and rode after the French. The Emir did not go with them. He left Gemalfin, a soldier he could trust, in command, and rode off with an escort of four dukes to Saragossa.

As soon as he reached the palace, he dismounted on to a marble stone while one of the dukes held the stirrup for him. He was half-way up the long staircase that led to King Marsila's room when Queen Bramimunde came running down towards him and threw herself at his feet.

'My lord is dying—dying in shame and misery!' she cried. 'What have we done to deserve this?'

The Emir stooped to help her to her feet and gently led her up to the King's room. She was almost out of her mind with grief.

King Marsila opened his eyes and saw the Emir gazing anxiously down at him. In a voice that was little more than a whisper he called for two attendants.

'Lift me in your arms,' he said. 'Help me to sit up.'

Propped against his pillows, he reached with his left hand—his only hand—for one of his gloves, and held it up for Baligant to take.

'My Lord Emir and King,' he said, 'I return to you all my lands and kingdoms, and Saragossa my beloved capital.' With a sigh of infinite sadness, he added, 'I have lost my honour and my good name. I have lost all my people.'

'I grieve for you, sir. My heart goes out to you,' said the Emir. 'I wish I could stay and talk longer, but Charlemagne will not wait. Thank you for your glove and your gift—I will try to deserve them.'

Unable to hide his feelings, he turned away; then hurried down the steps to rejoin his escort.

As they galloped along the crowded streets, the pagans scattered before them. Through the ten gates, over the four bridges they went, riding like the mountain wind, and in no time they had caught up with their army. Eager to take his place at the front, the Emir galloped past them, shouting at the top of his voice, 'Forward into battle! The French are on the run! The French are on the run!'

XIII

Honouring the Dead

WHILE THE DAWN mist lay like a coverlet
over the sleeping French army, Charlemagne awoke. And St Gabriel, who had
stood all night at his head watching over him, raised
his hand and made the sign of the cross on him as

he lay there on the ground among his soldiers.
Charlemagne rose and, stripping off his white mailcoat with the purple border, ordered his whole army
to take off their armour before resuming the march.
They mounted their horses and rode briskly over
the plains and through the long winding valleys till
they came to Roncesvalles.

'Draw in your reins now, my lord barons,' he
said. 'I am going on alone to find my nephew—he
cannot be far from here. I remember something
he once told me, at Aix on a feast day. My knights
were boasting of their deeds in battle when suddenly
Roland spoke of his death. He said he would die in
a foreign land far beyond his friends, with his face
towards the enemy.'

He spurred his horse forward and cantered uphill.
The wild flowers all round him were red, the seed-
clusters of the waving grasses were red—red with
the blood of his soldiers. And he wept for them.

He came to a pine tree and four boundary stones
of gleaming marble. There was a shattered rock
nearby, and when he looked at the pieces he knew
that only Roland could have struck such blows. A
moment later he saw him lying there on the cool
grass, with his sword and his broken horn under
him and his face towards Spain. Above him rose
the tree, above the tree the white peaks of the
mountains, above the mountains the burning sky.

With a cry he leapt down from his horse and took
Roland's head between his hands. Dazed with grief,
he swooned away. When he came to his senses, four
barons were holding him in their arms. They helped

him to his feet and left him leaning against the trunk of the tree, gazing down on Roland's body. How firm and shapely the limbs looked! But the flesh was pale and lustreless, the eyes full of darkness.

Very gently he called Roland's name and spoke to him as tenderly as words could.

'God have mercy on you, Roland. May your soul find rest in the flowered fields of Paradise. I sent you to Spain to your death, and I shall mourn you all the days of my life. I have no kinsman to match you, not a friend in all the world. All my strength and gladness are gone.'

He plucked his white beard and his long white hair, and a hundred thousand Frenchmen mourned with him.

'I will go back to France,' he said. 'When I am in my chapel at Aix, men will come from far countries for news of you. And I shall tell them, "My nephew made me great—and he is dead." Now the Saxons will rise up against me, the Hungarians and Bulgars, the Romans and Apulians. The black hordes of Africa will swoop down upon me. There will be no end to my tribulations. I wish I were lying on the field with my knights. I wish my soul could dwell with their souls, and my flesh be buried with their flesh.'

He plucked his white beard and his long white hair, and a hundred thousand Frenchmen swooned on the ground.

'I have never seen such grief—he will lose his reason,' said Duke Naimon.

'Lord Emperor, I beg you to be calm,' said

Geoffrey of Anjou. 'Let us search the field for our
dead and bury them in a common grave.'

'It shall be done,' said the Emperor. 'Blow your
horn.'

At the sound of the horn the French dismounted.
Some began to dig the grave while others searched
for their friends' bodies. Among them they found
many bishops and abbots, monks and canons and
priests with shaven crowns; and they absolved and
blessed them in God's Name. They burnt myrrh
and incense and laid them in the grave. They
raised a great burial mound above them.

Roland, Oliver and Archbishop Turpin were not
in the grave with the rest. They had been kept
apart, as the Emperor wished to do them special
honour. He had their hearts wrapped in white silk
and put in a marble urn, their bodies washed in
wine and spices and wound in shrouds of deerskin.
Then he chose four of his barons and said, 'Put the
bodies on three wagons and watch over them.'

While the soldiers were busy with their tasks, the
Emperor, his mind clouded with sad contemplation,
did not notice a party of horsemen riding towards
him. Two messengers had detached themselves from
the main body and dismounted in front of him
before he was aware of their presence.

'Who are you and what is your business?' he
asked. And he marvelled at their gaudy barbarian
trappings and their haughty looks.

'Proud Emperor, we are from Baligant,' said the
taller of the two, a Syrian with a pointed black beard.
'We bring you his challenge to fight him today.'

'He is behind you on the other side of the hill, and with him all the power and might of Arabia,' said the other messenger, who was a Persian. 'His armies stand between you and France. You have no hope of escaping now.'

They smiled at Charlemagne with triumph and contempt in their eyes, as if victory were already theirs.

XIV

Christians and Pagans prepare for Battle

THE EMPEROR STROKED his beard thoughtfully as he considered the messengers' words. He remembered Roland and Oliver and the lost rearguard. Now there was Baligant to face —a greater man than Marsila, a more dangerous enemy, and master of many kingdoms beyond the

sea. To defeat him would mean not only avenging
Roland but striking a blow in defence of Christendom. At once his gloom vanished.

'Go back to your Emir and tell him I accept his
challenge and will destroy him,' he said. Then,
turning to his army, he cried out in a loud voice,
'To horse, my lord barons! To arms!'

Quickly he put on his coat of mail, laced up his
helmet and buckled his sword Joyous to his side—
how it flashed and sparkled in the sun! Hanging
his shield round his neck, he grasped his spear
firmly and tossed it high into the air. He was ready
for battle long before anyone else. Then he mounted
Wildfire, the horse he had won at the ford of Mar-
sonne when he hurled Malpallin from the saddle.
He shook the bridle free, he spurred him hard, he
made him prance and gallop. And a hundred thousand Frenchmen cheered him till the mountains
rang.

'They are fine soldiers, Duke Naimon. I can trust
them to the death,' he said, as he watched them
put on their armour and mount their horses.
'These Arabs will be sorry they ever crossed the
water. They shall pay dearly for Roland.'

'God grant they may,' said Duke Naimon.

The Emperor called Rabel and his companion
Guinemant to him.

'Gentlemen, you are to take over the commands
that Roland and Oliver held,' he said. 'You shall
have fifteen thousand Frenchmen under you—
young knights, the bravest in the land. Rabel, here
is Roland's sword. Guinemant, you shall have his

ivory horn. Now ride, both of you, to the head of your company.'

As the company moved off, their painted spears shining in the sun, their pennons gallant as a field of nodding flowers, another cheer rang out.

Then the Emperor and Duke Naimon assembled nine divisions and sent them to battle stations on either wing. They were drawn from all over western Europe—from Bavaria, Germany, Holland, Normandy, Auvergne, Poitou, Brittany, Lorraine and Burgundy. The Emperor himself took the centre, with the tenth division—a hundred thousand strong—under his personal command. They were all barons of France, war veterans, greybeards with grizzled hair, straight of limb and haughty in their bearing. Their breastplates were of double mail, their swords of French and Spanish steel, and their shields painted with various devices. In front Geoffrey of Anjou carried the standard, the red banner of St Peter.

The Emperor dismounted and knelt down on the grass to pray. He lifted his face towards the rising sun and from the stronghold of his heart called out to God:

'True Father in Heaven, watch over me today. Thou didst save Jonah in the whale's belly. Thou didst deliver Daniel from the lions and the three children from the raging fire. Surround me now with Thy love and, if it be Thy will, grant that I may avenge my nephew Roland!'

His prayer ended, he stood up and crossed himself. Duke Naimon held the stirrup while he mounted, then handed him his shield and spear of ashwood. How magnificent he looked! His eyes were radiant, his body erect as the straightest, tallest fir tree, king of the forests in the far north. From in front and behind the trumpets sounded—and above them all rose the long melancholy wail of Roland's horn, reminding him of his loss, drawing tears from his eyes and from the eyes of every Frenchman there.

He brushed sorrow aside, spurred his horse and rode gallantly forward, his white beard spilling over his coat of mail and blowing in the breeze. And because they loved him a hundred thousand Frenchmen did as he did.

They passed the hills and the high mountains; they wound through the deep gorges and the narrow places of darkness and despair; they came out through the gates of the valleys, across the barren lands of Spain, and at last to a great plain that stretched as far as the eye could see. They knew that the pagan army could not be far away now. They were on fire to meet them.

Meanwhile Baligant's two scouts had returned to him.

'We have seen Charlemagne,' said the Syrian. 'His men are as stubborn as he is. They will never run. Put on your armour at once—you will have to fight them.'

Baligant's eyes flashed. 'Blow the trumpets and the bugles,' he commanded. 'Beat the drums of war.'

At once the pagans dismounted and put on their armour. The Emir fastened on his coat of mail with the sky-blue border, laced up his gold and jewelled helmet, and buckled his sword to his side—it was called Lightning, which was also his battle cry. Round his neck he hung his shield. It was bound with crystal and had a golden boss and a strap of thick silk embroidered with roses. His spear, which was called Warspite, was as thick as a beam, and the weight of its iron alone was a full load for a mule. Like Charlemagne, Baligant was ready long before the rest of his army.

While one of his knights held the stirrup, he mounted his Arab charger. How powerful he looked, with his broad shoulders, his deep chest and long straight back; and his huge legs seemed to straddle his horse like a Colossus. His hair was white as curling foam, and his face like the raging sea. What a knight he would have made had he been a Christian!

There was a ditch in front of him some fifty feet wide. Spurring his charger till the blood spurted from its side, with a great curving leap he cleared it at a single bound.

The pagans cheered him, shouting, 'There is no one in the world to match Baligant. Charlemagne was mad to stay in Spain.'

'He will take to his heels the moment he sees us,' said the Emir's son, Malpramis, who was as stalwart and massive as his father.

'Charlemagne is a man of honour—he will not run away,' said Baligant. 'But without Roland where are the tiger's claws? My Syrian scout tells me the Emperor is advancing on us with ten divisions. The vanguard are fifteen thousand strong, all of them picked men—the Emperor calls them his sons—and Guinemant and Rabel are in command. One of them has Roland's horn and the other his sword, but what can they do without Roland? I wouldn't give a glove for either of them.'

'Sir, may I have the honour of striking the first blow?' said Malpramis.

'Willingly,' said Baligant. 'The King of Persia shall go with you and the King of Lycia too. If you can grind these French braggarts in the dust, I'll give you half my kingdoms.' And so confident was he of success that he gave him the titles there and then.

'I thank you with all my heart,' said Malpramis, as he received them from his father—the kingdoms he was never to see.

With Malpramis and the two Kings close behind him, Baligant rode off to inspect his army. Altogether he had thirty divisions, the smallest of which was fifty thousand strong. They were drawn from all over the pagan world—as far east as the steppes of Russia, as far west as the Sahara. They included Turks, Persians, Nubians, Huns, Hungarians, men of Baghdad and Jericho, negroes from Ethiopia, Slavs and Armenians, towering giants from Malprise, and wild-beards from Fronde who hated God. From Occian in the desert came a tribe whose skins were so iron-hard that they needed no helmets or chain mail, and from Myconia creatures with monstrous heads and with the bristles of wild boars sprouting from their spines. A savage, godless and gigantic army.

Well pleased with his divisions, the Emir rode to the front. His dragon standard was carried before him, as well as the banners of his three gods— Termagant, Mohammed and foul Apollyon. Ten Canaanites rode with him, shouting their gospel and crying, 'Bow down to our gods, pray to them and they will protect you.'

Meanwhile the French army was approaching. From the far side of the plain they heard the shouting. As the pagans dutifully bowed their heads, they

saw a hundred thousand helmets sweep the ground
and turn to flashing diamonds in the sunlight. They
shook their spears at the pagans and cried, 'Idola-
ters! We put our trust in the living God. He will
be our strength and shield. Your gods are false and
will utterly confound you.'

To Baligant these words were like the beating of
raindrops on rock. He was unmoved. A courageous
leader and no fool in the art of war, he calmly called
his son and the two Kings over to him.

'You are to ride at the head of all my divisions,'
he told them, 'all except three—the Turks, the
Ormalian knights, and the giants from Malprise.
I mean to hold these in reserve. I shall keep the
wild desert tribesmen from Occian to grapple with
Charlemagne and the French centre, and I will
lead them myself.'

He looked across the plain to the French position. Both armies could see each other clearly. There was no hill or valley, no wood or lurking-place between them, only a narrow strip of open country. This was the only ground visible. As far as the sky-rim nothing else could be seen but golden helmets and blazoned shields, flowered pennons and blue-bordered coats of mail—a tapestry of dazzling colour.

The standard-bearer lifted the Dragon high into the air. As they watched it clawing the wind and breathing out fire from its tongue, the pagans cheered and shouted again and again. The French replied by shouting 'Mountjoy!' their battle cry. They sounded the trumpets as well as Roland's horn, whose freezing note rang out loud and clear above all the din. The pagans trembled when they

heard it and muttered to each other, 'Roland is dead, but his spirit still lives. The battle will be hard and long.'

Then Baligant called his brother Canabeus and pointed out to him the French divisions and the Emperor riding proudly between the ranks. 'They are veteran troops,' he said, 'arrogant, with beards white as driven snow—that spill over their coats of mail and blow in the breeze. What a battle it will be! We shall beat them to their knees, we shall grind them in the dust.'

He rode out beyond his army about the length of a spear's flight when a strong man hurls it, then called back over his shoulder, 'Sons of darkness, ride on! Follow me!'

And shaking the great shaft of his spear, he pointed the iron tip at Charlemagne's heart.

The Emperor did not flinch. He stood calmly watching, still and motionless as a mountain peak. He looked at the Dragon shuddering in the wind and at the vast Arabian army sprawled over the land right to the sky-rim.

'These pagans are numberless as the waves of the sea,' he said. 'But who cares? If there are any cowards among us, they can go home—I shall ride without them.'

He spurred his horse Wildfire and four times, in huge curves of splendour, it leapt into the air.

And the French cried out in wonder, 'God in Heaven, here is an Emperor for all the world to envy! Sir, we shall not fail you. Ride on!'

XV

The Last Battle

THE FIERCE SUN beat down on the two armies
as they faced each other on the plain. They
were ready for battle.

Levelling their spears for the charge, Rabel and
Guinemant gave rein to their running horses and
spurred them hard. Rabel drove his spear through
the King of Persia's body. Guinemant overthrew

the King of Lycia, shattering his shield, ripping his coat of mail and smiting him dead.

The French cheered them and shouted, 'You see, barons—God is on our side. Forward into battle!'

As they charged, the pagans stood their ground. And the armies clashed together with the shock of seas meeting, the tumultuous mingling of great waters. In the buffet and swirl of battle, what splintering of spears there was, what smashing of shields, what rending of mailcoats! The ground was strewn with mangled armour, and the grass ran red with blood.

Through the press rode a white horse with Malpramis in the saddle, hewing to right and to left
while Frenchmen fell by the score.

'My lords,' said Baligant, with fatherly pride,
'see how defiantly he rides, this son of mine. I could
not wish for a braver soldier. Remember all the
years I have looked after you and fed you on the
fat of the land—help him now with your cutting
spears.'

The pagans surged forward to help him and were
sucked into the swell of battle.

'Sons of darkness, strike and strike again!'

shouted Baligant. 'I'll give you lands and lovely
women, I'll load you with honours and riches.'

They laid about them so furiously that they broke
their spears. Then a hundred thousand swords
flashed in their hands, and grim and terrible was
the slaughter.

'My lord barons,' said Charlemagne, 'I love you
and trust you. You have fought my battles for me,
won me my kingdoms and overthrown kings. Without you I should be worth nothing. I owe you my
lands, my wealth and life itself. It is not long since
your sons and brothers fell at Roncesvalles. The
time has come to avenge them, for we know that
God is on our side.'

Twenty thousand Frenchmen answered, 'We
shall not fail you. We shall fight to the death.'

With spears and with swords and with the thunder
of their horses they hurled themselves at the pagans.

But nothing seemed to daunt Malpramis. On he
rode through the middle of the field, unchecked,
dealing what ruin he would—till Duke Naimon
caught up with him. He lunged into the Prince like
a battering-ram, smashing his shield-rim, tearing
the hem of his mailcoat, and thrusting his spear-
point and yellow pennon right into his flesh. And
he threw him down among seven hundred corpses.

The Duke had barely withdrawn his spear when
King Canabeus, the Emir's brother, was upon him.
He brought his crystal-hilted sword crashing down
on to Naimon's helmet, splitting it down one side
and cutting through the lacing. The blow stunned
him, but he managed to throw his arms round his

horse's neck and cling on. Canabeus lifted his sword for the final blow, but suddenly, at this moment of mortal peril, God sent Charlemagne to help Naimon.

'Son of a slave, you shall pay for this,' said the Emperor. And aiming his spear at the King's heart, he drove right through his shield and killed him in one blow.

He turned to Duke Naimon. When he saw his friend, so dazed and wounded, struggling painfully to sit his horse, while the grass below him ran red with blood, his eyes were full of compassion. He reached out to help him and spoke to him as gently as words could.

'Naimon, my noble friend, keep close to my side. The brute who nearly killed you is dead. I ran him through with my spear.'

'Sir, I owe you my life,' said Duke Naimon. 'As long as I live, I shall never forget it.'

Sustained by the love and loyalty that bound them, they rode back into the press together. And twenty thousand Frenchmen fought on at their side.

Unaware of his son's death, Baligant rode confidently through the field, seeking out captains and champions. When he found Guinemant, he rode full tilt at him with his spear, shattering his white shield, tearing his mailcoat, and hurling him dead from his galloping horse. Next he struck down Geboin and Lorant and Richard the Old, Lord of Normandy.

The pagans shouted, 'Lightning is mighty and strong in wonders. Strike, barons, and strike again!'

Then Baligant called on the knights of Arabia and Arguille and the wild lords of Occian, whose skins were so iron-hard that they needed no helmets or chain mail, and he pitted them against the French centre. God in Heaven, what a battle it was! You should have seen the cut and thrust of their spears. You should have heard the shield-smashing, the ring of iron on helmets, the harsh grating as mail-rings ripped.

But the French lines stood firm. All day long, through morning and noon and the slanting shadows they laboured, while knights, hurled from a thousand saddles, lay groaning and dying on the ground. Was there ever such suffering in the world before?

Then Baligant in his vanity cried out to Mohammed

and Termagant and foul Apollyon, 'My lord gods, I have served you faithfully. Give me victory and I will make you images of fine gold—oh, give me victory!'

His hands were still clasped in prayer when a messenger ran up and flung himself at his feet.

'Sir, I bring you bad news. Your son Malpramis and your brother Canabeus are both killed. I think the Emperor himself killed one of them. Though he is old and his beard is white as the may-blossom, he is no weakling. He is raging through the field like a lion.'

Baligant bowed his head and he turned his face, dark with sadness, to the ground. Then he called for Jangleu, his counsellor from over the sea.

'Be honest with me, Jangleu,' he said. 'I have always leaned on your advice. How is the battle going? Can we win?'

And Jangleu answered bitterly, 'Baligant, you are as good as dead. Your gods will not shield you. Charlemagne is too proud to yield, his men are brave beyond all praise—I've never seen such fighters. You must call your reserves—your Turks and Africans, your giants from Malprise, the men of Arguille and the wild lords from Occian in the desert. Waste not a moment.'

Baligant was no coward. Unafraid of being seen, he spread out his beard, white as curling foam, over his mailcoat. Then he put a trumpet to his lips and blew a long shrill call.

At once the pagans rallied. The men of Arguille yelped like dogs, the desert lords of Occian brayed and whinnied. As a mountain avalanche at the spring melting, they swept down on the French and broke them and crushed them and trampled seven thousand dead.

When he saw what had happened, Count Oger of Denmark, commander of the Bavarian division, summoned Thierry Duke of Argonne, Geoffrey of Anjou and Count Jozeran. He turned on Charlemagne, his eyes blazing with reproach.

'Sir, will you stand by while the pagans wreck your army? Fly to your vengeance, wipe out the disgrace, or may God smite the crown from your head!'

In the shocked silence no one dared say a word.

Then the French, with Geoffrey of Anjou in front waving the Red Banner of St Peter, gave rein to their running horses and charged. They could see the pagan Dragon streaming in the wind high above the Arab helmets. As the lines clashed together, Charlemagne and Duke Naimon laid about them with ringing blows. Suddenly a channel opened in the press, and Count Oger dashed into it. He rode full tilt at the standard-bearer and cut him down. He lopped the wooden shaft and stamped the Dragon in the dust.

Baligant shuddered, his huge frame trembled. Were his gods, he wondered, false gods? Could Charlemagne be right?

And the pagans of Arabia, sick with fear, held back.

'My lord barons,' cried Charlemagne, 'help me now for the love of God!'

'We need no asking,' said the French. 'We shall fight to the death.'

The shadows lengthened, the day mellowed into evening; and still the battle raged, still the shouts of 'Lightning!' and 'Mountjoy!' split the air.

Clear above the rest rose the voices of Baligant and Charlemagne. Each could hear the other, and they charged and clashed together in mid-field in a flurry of steel. They drove their spears into their rose-stippled shields and broke them under the broad bosses. They ripped the hems of their coats of mail, but did not reach their bodies. Then the saddle-girths snapped, the pommels slipped sideways, and both Kings thudded to the ground. The horses kicked free of the tangled harness and galloped off. Springing to their feet, the two Kings drew their swords.

Oh, how the white blades flashed as they struck and struck at their shields! They cut through the leather and the double-wood frame, they burst the rivets and broke the bosses. With no shields to save them now, they hammered at their mailcoats. Under the glancing steel, their helmets sparkled with fire. They knew there could be no ending now till one of them lay dead.

'Charlemagne, there is still time for you to repent,' said Baligant. 'You killed my son, you seized my lands. Bow to me and I'll be your liege-lord. Come and serve me from Spain to my kingdoms in the east.'

'What, stoop to treachery?' said Charlemagne. 'How could I yield to a pagan? Confess first to the

Christian faith, then I will be your friend. God
Omnipotent is the King to serve.'

'Blasphemy!' said Baligant.

And again the swords flashed out.

Then Baligant with tremendous force brought
Lightning crashing down on the Emperor's helmet,
splitting it and shaving from his face a strip of flesh
as wide as his hand. The cheek was bare to the bone.

Charlemagne stumbled and nearly fell. But God
did not intend him to be killed. Dazed, staggering
with weariness, he looked up from the field and
saw an angel hovering between him and the setting
sun. In the shadow of the wing-spread he heard St
Gabriel call him.

'Great King, why do you falter? Rise up and fight again.'

And Charlemagne drew strength from the angel's presence. Fearless of death, renewed in spirit, he lifted his sword Joyous and brought it ringing down on Baligant's helmet. He cut through the gems of fire, he shattered the steel, and shouting 'Mountjoy!' struck him down dead.

At the Emperor's cry of triumph Duke Naimon came running to him, leading Wildfire by the rein. Charlemagne mounted, and with a yell of despair the pagans turned and fled. Their leader was down. The French had won the day.

'My lords,' said Charlemagne, 'forget your sorrows—they belong to yesterday. Lift up your hearts, rejoice! And ride to your revenge!'

And like the whirlwind that carries all in its path, they swept the pagans far over the darkening plain.

XVI

The Return Home

ALL NIGHT THEY chased them, and all the next
day—in the torturing heat and choking dust—
as far as Saragossa. From the top of her tower
Queen Bramimunde saw the great cloud of dust
that heralded their coming. She was surrounded by
her clerks and canons, priests of pagan law with
unshaven crowns and no spiritual orders, all watching anxiously as the swelling cloud moved nearer.
When she saw the Arabs in wild disorder, and

Charlemagne beating down the city gates, she cried out to Mohammed to help—then ran to the vaulted room where King Marsila lay dying.

'Noble King, our armies are routed and the Emir killed,' she said. 'We are ruined.'

When Marsila heard her, the tears burst from his eyes. Crushed with sorrow and mortified with shame, he turned his haggard face to the wall and died. And the Devil took his soul to hell.

So Marsila's city, with its ten great towers and fifty turrets, passed into the hands of Charlemagne. He sent a thousand Frenchmen into the mosques and synagogues to break up the images and wipe out all trace of idolatry. He gave orders that any pagans who refused to become Christian should be thrown into the dungeons or burned alive. Altogether more than a hundred thousand were baptized, but not Queen Bramimunde. Charlemagne had decided to take her back to France as a prisoner and to try to win her to the Faith by persuasion and not by force. That night he and his army, proud in their God-given victory, slept within the city walls. And the moon and the stars shone peacefully upon them.

In the first light of morning, leaving a garrison of a thousand knights, he set off with his army on the long journey home. Queen Bramimunde rode beside him, for his heart was merciful towards her and he wished her no harm. And there was much gladness and rejoicing.

For one man—Ganelon—there was no rejoicing. Still riding his pack-horse, closely guarded, chained by the neck, pounded and cudgelled on the slightest provocation, he trailed ignominiously along at the rear of the army.

The huge host moved on across the great plain and the barren lands of Spain, through the gates of the valleys, through the deep gorges and the narrow places of darkness and despair, over the high passes of the Pyrenees, right to the Gates of France. One morning they woke to see their beloved country stretched out before them, clear and green and lovely in the growing light. And every heart but Ganelon's leapt with joy. Like homing swallows near the end of their long journey, wing-weary, chastened by the wind and the storm, they were happy beyond measure and at peace with themselves.

At Bordeaux they filled Roland's horn with gold sovereigns and left it under the altar of St Severin, where pilgrims who visit the place may see it still. Crossing the River Gironde, with its sparkling waters and delicate white-winged ships, they came to Blaye. Here, at the church of St Romayne, they buried the bodies of Roland and Oliver and Archbishop Turpin in sumptuous white tombs, commending their souls to Almighty God.

There were no more delays, and the Emperor hurried back over the length and breadth of France to his capital, Aix, on the eastern border. Dismounting at the palace gates, he climbed the long flight of steps and went into the hall.

And Alda the beautiful, Oliver's sister and Roland's betrothed, came running to him.

'Where is Roland?' she asked. 'He promised to wed me when he came back.'

The Emperor's face turned grey with sorrow. Tears burst from his eyes and he plucked his white beard.

'Sister, gentle lady, he is dead,' said Charlemagne. 'I will give you Louis in his place—my son Louis, heir to my kingdom and very dear to my heart.'

'Your words mean nothing to me,' said Alda. 'How can I go on living now Roland is dead?'

The colour faded from her cheeks and she fell at his feet.

Thinking she had fainted, he knelt down and took her by the hands and lifted her up. Her head fell back, her long flaxen hair flowed over his shoulder. With deep compassion he gazed into her face, white and lovely as snow on high mountains. There was no flicker of life at all. Softly he called her name, but she had gone where no voice could call her back.

Four countesses carried her to a convent, where they watched over her body all night until the coming of day. And they buried her beside an altar, with all the solemnity and honour due to her gentle name.

XVII

The Trial of Ganelon

DRAGGING ALONG ON his pack-horse at the rear of the French army, sullen-faced, stung by the insults flung at him and grimy from the dust of the road, Ganelon was the last of the long cavalcade to reach Aix. As soon as he came to the palace, he was pulled off his horse and tugged by the chain into the courtyard. Servants and kitchen knaves tied him to a stake and bound his hands with leather straps. They beat him with sticks and cudgels and left him there, snarling with hurt pride, to await his trial.

Meanwhile the Emperor had sent messengers all over his kingdom to find judges who were experienced and trustworthy enough to try the case. With all speed they came from every corner of his realm—from Bavaria to Brittany, from Holland to Lorraine, and from the heart of France as well. On the feast day of St Silvester they assembled in the Great Hall at Aix, and the trial of Ganelon began.

'My lord barons,' said Charlemagne, 'I ask you to hear my charges against Ganelon and to judge which of us is right. He was with my army in Spain. There he betrayed my Twelve Peers and lost twenty thousand of my Frenchmen. Thanks to his murderous scheming you will never see my nephew Roland again nor brave and courteous Oliver. Why did he do this? I say it was out of greed and jealousy.'

Ganelon stood up and faced the Emperor. In spite of the humiliations he had suffered, he had lost none of his spirit and was as pert and resilient as ever.

'I'm not ashamed of anything I've done,' he said. 'Roland swindled me out of money and estate. I had every cause to plot his death and disgrace. I can see no treason in that.'

The judges were perplexed. 'This is no simple matter of right and wrong,' they said. 'We must consider it carefully.'

Ganelon looked up at the judges on their high-backed chairs, then down into the court where the

French and thirty of his kinsmen, who had come to support him, were sitting.

'Listen to me, my lords, for the love of God,' he said, and his voice rang loud and clear and defiant as a trumpet-call. 'I was in the Emperor's army, and I served him faithfully and well. But Roland hated me bitterly, and you know what he did. He forced me to go as envoy to that butcher Marsila. What else was this but base conspiracy? He meant to have me murdered. If I had not kept my wits about me, I should never have come back alive. Roland was not only a braggart—we all know that —but a swindler and a murderer too. So I defied him. I defied Oliver and the other Peers, the whole pack of them. I took my revenge. But the quarrel was between me and the man who wronged me, and I did nothing treasonable.'

With his head in the air, Ganelon swept back to his seat. There was a stir in the court and much murmuring against him. On the faces of his kinsmen there were passionate looks, and on their lips the clamour of fierce words.

'We shall hold our council now,' said the judges. And they retired to the far end of the Great Hall.

While they were busy debating, Ganelon strode over to talk to his kinsmen. Their leader was Pinabel, lord of the castle of Sorence, a brave soldier and an eloquent, quick-witted speaker.

'Pinabel,' he said, and, for all his swagger, there was more than a hint of uneasiness in his voice, 'you must get me out of this. I don't want to be killed.'

'You are perfectly safe,' said Pinabel. 'If any

Frenchman should sentence you to hanging, I'd challenge him to meet me in the lists. My spear and my sword would soon prove him false.'

Ganelon smiled with relief. He went down on his knees and kissed Pinabel's feet. Then he got up and, still smiling, glanced at the far end of the council chamber where the judges were debating. They spoke in hushed voices, for they were afraid of Pinabel.

'The charge of treachery has not been proved,' they were saying. 'Is there any point in going on with the trial? It would be wiser to abandon it and ask the Emperor to release Ganelon. He should be given a chance to show his loyalty. Roland is dead and we shall never see him again. All the gold in the world cannot bring him back. As for Pinabel, only a fool would choose to quarrel with him.'

This was the general view. Thierry, Geoffrey of Anjou's brother, was the only one who did not share it.

The judges rose and went over to Charlemagne.

'Sir, we ask you to release Ganelon,' they said. 'He comes of noble family and can still prove himself your loyal servant. You have nothing to gain by killing him. All the gold in the world cannot bring Roland back.'

'You are traitors and cowards!' said the Emperor. He bowed his head, and his brow was dark as thunder.

At once Thierry stood up. He was lean and straight of limb, neither short nor tall, with dark skin and black hair. He spoke with grave courtesy.

'My lord and Emperor, do not distress yourself,' he said. 'I have always served you well, and I feel it my duty to speak out now. Roland may have wronged Ganelon, but what of that? He was serving you at the time—you, his Emperor—and his person was therefore sacred. In betraying Roland, Ganelon was doubly false—false to Roland and false to you, sir. I say he should hang for this. His body—for he's no better than a common criminal—should be dragged in the dust. Is there anyone here who disputes my judgement? If there is, I can prove it true with this,' and he slapped the hilt of his sword.

'Bravely spoken!' cried the French.

There was a great clamour of voices, many of them shouting for Thierry, but Ganelon's kinsmen looked violent and dangerous and were noisiest of all.

Then Pinabel sprang to his feet. He was a bigger man than Thierry, stalwart, broad-shouldered, nimble on his toes. He had only to strike a man once and that was the end of him.

'My lord Emperor, this is your court,' he said, with a contemptuous wave of the hand. 'The din is disgraceful. Are you so feeble that you cannot stop it? What business has Thierry to call himself a judge? He's a liar. I challenge him to meet me in the lists.' As a pledge of honour he handed the Emperor his deerskin glove.

'Here is my answer,' said Thierry. His eyes flashing, he handed the Emperor his own glove.

'We must have sureties,' said Charlemagne. 'I

am willing to stand for Thierry. Who will stand for Pinabel?'

'We will,' said his thirty kinsmen, and they stood on the benches and shouted their leader's name.

As soon as he had fixed a time for the combat, the Emperor put Ganelon's kinsmen under close guard as pledges for Pinabel's appearance in the lists. He ordered these to be set up in the Champions' Field outside the city walls. Four benches were brought for the combatants and their sureties, and Count Oger of Denmark was appointed Marshall to settle the procedure.

Before the combat, Thierry and Pinabel both attended Mass and received the Sacrament. Among the flickering candles of the Emperor's chapel, in the incense-heavy air, they prayed to God that the outcome of the fight would reveal which of them was right. Then, leaving behind them generous gifts for the monasteries, they called for their horses and armour and went straight to the lists, where Charlemagne was waiting.

The hour for the Trial by Combat had arrived.

They put on their spurs and white coats of mail, they laced up their helmets and buckled to their sides their gold-hilted swords. From their necks they hung their quartered shields and, spear in hand, mounted their horses. Thierry looked much smaller and slighter than Pinabel. A hundred thousand knights were watching, and their hearts ached for him.

At a given signal the two riders set their spears in rest. Loosening their reins, spurring hard, they charged. They thundered over the turf and clashed together. So mighty was the impact that they smashed their shields, they ripped their coats of mail, they broke their saddle-girths. The high saddles twisted and tumbled to the ground, dragging both knights with them, while the shocked horses galloped away.

Lightly they leapt to their feet and fell upon each other with their swords. They hacked at their helmets till the splinters went flying.

'God champion the right!' said Charlemagne.

And the French cheered and shouted.

When Thierry stumbled and nearly fell, Pinabel called on him to surrender. 'I will serve you loyally,' he said. 'I will give you anything you ask if you will make peace between Ganelon and Charlemagne.'

Thierry refused with scorn. 'God must judge between you and me today,' he said. 'I like your courage, Pinabel. You are tough and strong of limb. Why waste your strength on me? I'll make your peace with Charlemagne, and Ganelon shall be punished as he deserves.'

'I prize my good name,' said Pinabel. 'I will not yield to any man alive.'

They struck again, and the flames danced on their jewelled helmets and leapt into the sky. There could be no ending now till one of them lay dead.

Was there ever a swordsman to match Pinabel? Down came the blade on Thierry's helmet, and a shower of crackling fire rained on the grass and set it blazing. Down it came again, cutting Thierry's

forehead and cheek and one side of his mailcoat.
But God held him from falling.

The blood streamed down Thierry's face on to
the burning grass. He was so dazed he could hardly
see. Gathering the last of his failing strength, he
lifted his sword high in the air and struck once more
at Pinabel's helmet. He split it down the nose-piece
and the blow killed him. Thierry had won.

The French were wild with delight. Their cheers
rang to high Heaven. 'God has done a miracle,'
they cried. 'In the name of justice, Ganelon and
his thirty kinsmen must hang.'

Stunned and exhausted, Thierry could hardly
keep upright. The Emperor ran to him and took
him in his arms. Tenderly with his great marten fur
he wiped the blood and sweat from his face. The
French knights crowded round. With gentle fingers
they disarmed him, for his flesh was bruised and
torn. Then they put a cloak round his shoulders and
mounted him on an Arab mule. And he went back
to the city in triumph like a conqueror and dismounted in the square.

At once Charlemagne assembled all his counts
and dukes in the Great Hall. He raised his hand
for silence.

'Thirty kinsmen of Ganelon's came to his trial
as hostages,' he said. 'I have them outside under
guard. What do you wish me to do with them?'

'Kill them,' said the French. 'It would be wrong
for them to live.'

'Send Basbrun to me,' said the Emperor. Basbrun
was Officer of the Guard, and when he arrived

Charlemagne commanded him, 'Go and hang them on the tree of doom. By my beard, if one of them escapes you shall die.'

The doors of the Great Hall closed behind him as he went off to do the Emperor's bidding. Some minutes later there was a great clamour in the street outside. Basbrun and a hundred soldiers of the Imperial Guard were marching away the kinsmen to be hanged.

Next the judges met to consider how Ganelon should die. The French judges were the most vindictive among them, and it was they who devised the manner of his death. They had his feet and hands tied to four horses. Then four sergeants led them to a field where a mare was running free—and let them loose. Away they sped with lightning paces and tore him limb from limb.

So Ganelon died and Roland was avenged.

So perish all traitors! They sow the seeds of destruction everywhere, they bring death to their kin and downfall to nations. They should not live to boast of their deeds.

XVIII

Charlemagne

THEN CHARLEMAGNE TURNED his face away
from all harshness and vengeance and summoned his bishops to his palace. They came
from Germany, Bavaria, and all over France.

'I have a prisoner in my house, a gentle, unhappy
lady,' he said. 'Her name is Bramimunde—once she
was Queen of Spain. She has been instructed in
Christian doctrine and is willing to believe in God

and walk in the ways of righteousness. Baptize her, that God may save her soul.'

'It shall be done,' they answered.

In the presence of a great multitude they baptized her by the waters of Aix and changed her name to Juliana.

Charlemagne was glad that she had of her own understanding turned Christian, glad too that with Ganelon's death justice had been done. So his load of anger was lightened. His aching heart, troubled for so long, was at last at peace, serene as the June sky.

Day passed into evening and evening into night. He was lying in his vaulted chamber when a rustling of wings in the darkness roused him from sleep. St Gabriel was beside his bed. He had come from God and was calling urgently, 'To arms, Charlemagne, to arms! Marshal your battalions, gather your might from the farthest corners of the empire and march into Elbira. King Vivian needs you— the pagans are besieging his city—the Christians in their agony cry out to you for help!'

Charlemagne heard him, and all his sorrow and weariness and despair surged back. He had no heart to go. He was very old, bowed down with the weight of his numbered years, and Roland's death had saddened him to the depths of his being.

'God,' he cried, 'how weary my life is, how heavy my soul!'

The tears burst from his eyes and he plucked his white beard.

Acknowledgements

THIS version is a retelling and not a literal translation. It is based on Bédier's edition of the Oxford MS of *Roland*. I have received valuable help from René Hague's prose translation (Faber and Faber Ltd, 1937), Dorothy Sayers's verse translation and commentary (Penguin Books, 1957), and Henri Chamard's translation into modern French (Librairie Armand Colin, 1948). My thanks are also due to my wife for much patient assistance, and to the artist Williams Stobbs for his spirited and distinguished drawings.